KU-077-416

Contents

Agatha Christie (1890-1976) is known throughout the world as the Queen of Crime. Her books have sold over a billion copies in English with another billion in over 100 foreign languages. She is the most widely published and translated author of all time and in any language; only the Bible and Shakespeare have sold more copies. She is the author of 80 crime novels and short story collections, 19 plays, and six other novels. *The Mousetrap*, her most famous play, was first staged in 1952 in London and is still performed there – it is the longest-running play in history.

Agatha Christie's first novel was published in 1920. It featured Hercule Poirot, the Belgian detective who has become the most popular detective in crime fiction since Sherlock Holmes. Collins has published Agatha Christie since 1926.

This series has been especially created for readers worldwide whose first language is not English. Each story has been shortened, and the vocabulary and grammar simplified to make it accessible to readers with a good intermediate knowledge of the language.

The following features are included after the story:

A **List of characters** to help the reader identify who is who, and how they are connected to each other. **Cultural notes** to explain historical and other references. A **Glossary** of words that some readers may not be familiar with are explained. There is also a Record

Agatha Christie

Death in the Clouds

Collins

Collins

HarperCollins Publishers
77-85 Fulham Palace Road
Hammersmith, London W6 8JB
www.collinselt.com

This *Collins English Readers Edition* published 2012

Reprint 10 9 8 7 6 5 4 3 2 1 0

Original text first published in Great Britain by Collins 1935

ISBN: 978-0-00-745160-9

A catalogue record for this book is available from the British Library.

Educational Consultant: Fitch O'Connell

Cover by crushed.co.uk © HarperCollins/Agatha Christie Ltd 2008

Typeset by Aptara in India

Printed and bound in Great Britain by Clays Ltd, St Ives plc

Chapter 1 Paris to Croydon

The September sun shone on Le Bourget airport near Paris as the passengers entered the aeroplane *Prometheus*, for their flight to England. Jane Grey went to her seat in the <u>rear</u> cabin, at the back of the plane.

A woman was standing nearby, talking very loudly. 'My dear Cicely! *Where* were you staying? Juan les Pins? Oh, yes. No, I've been in Le Pinet. Let's sit together. Oh, can't we? I see . . .'

A foreign voice said politely, 'Please, Madame, take my seat,' and a small, elderly man with a large moustache and an egg-shaped head got up from his seat.

Jane looked at the two women for whom he had offered to move to a different seat. She had also been staying at Le Pinet, a popular holiday destination on the French coast, and she remembered one of the women standing nervously at a table in the casino. Her name was Lady Horbury. She was married to a Lord now, but she had once been a dancer in musical and comedy theatre. Unlike Lady Horbury, the other woman clearly looked like a real <u>aristocrat</u>.

Jane turned to look out of the window. She would not look at the young man who was sitting opposite her. If their eyes met, he might recognize her from that night at the casino! She felt shy and embarrassed in front of him.

At last, the plane took off, and there was Le Bourget <u>spread out</u> below them. The midday flight to London carried twenty-one passengers – ten in the front cabin, eleven in the rear, and there were two stewards on board to look after everyone. As the plane flew towards the <u>English Channel</u>, Jane thought about her adventure. It started when she had won a hundred pounds in a <u>lottery</u> and decided to spend the money on a week at Le Pinet. Jane worked at a hairdressing salon called *Antoine's*, and her customers were always going down to Le Pinet. As Jane styled the hair of these rich and glamorous ladies, she thought, 'Why can't *I* go to Le Pinet?' Well, now she could. And so, she had.

Every evening of her holiday, Jane had gone to the casinos with a small amount of money to spend at the <u>gambling</u> tables. On her fourth evening, she decided to play at the <u>roulette wheel</u>. She won a little money, but lost more. As she waited to <u>place</u> her last <u>bet</u> of the evening, she saw that there were two numbers left which nobody had chosen: five and six. Which one would she choose?

The wheel began to spin, and Jane quickly placed her bet on number six. The ball clicked and settled.

'*Le numéro cinq, rouge,*' said the <u>croupier</u>.

Number five! Jane could have cried with disappointment.

Then the man next to her asked, 'Aren't you going to collect the money you have won?'

'What money? I bet on number six!'

'No, you bet on five.'

Was it true? Perhaps she had. She picked up her money and looked <u>doubtfully</u> at the stranger.

'Well done,' he said, and with a friendly smile, he left. And now here was that same man, sitting opposite her on the plane to England . . .

★

Across the cabin, Lady Horbury noticed that she had a broken fingernail, and asked the steward to fetch her maid, who was in the other cabin. Soon, a dark-haired French girl, dressed in black, appeared.

'Madeleine, fetch my little red case,' said Lady Horbury.

The maid went to the pile of suitcases at the end of the cabin and returned with a red leather case. Cicely Horbury sent her away, and took a <u>nail file</u> from the case.

★

Jane looked around the cabin. The little foreigner with the moustache was wrapped up in a blanket. His eyes were closed. Beside him sat a tall, grey-haired man. He looked like a <u>lawyer</u> or a doctor. Behind these men were two Frenchmen, talking excitedly.

Opposite Jane, Norman Gale was thinking, 'She definitely remembers me. She looked so disappointed when she lost the money she had bet in the casino. It was worth losing to see her pleasure when she won. I did that rather well. She's very attractive when she smiles . . .'

★

Now seated opposite Venetia Kerr, Lady Horbury thought to herself, 'Venetia Kerr always looks at me as if I was a piece of dirt. She wanted my husband Stephen for herself. Well, she didn't get him! But never mind about that – good heavens, what shall I do? That horrible old French woman meant what she said . . .'

Sitting opposite her, the <u>Honourable</u> Venetia Kerr thought, 'Little <u>tart</u>. Poor Stephen . . . if he could only <u>get rid of</u> her . . .'

★

Wrapped up in his blanket behind the ladies, Hercule Poirot looked at Jane and thought, 'That pretty little one. Why does she not look at the handsome young man opposite her . . . ?' The plane dropped slightly. '*Mon estomac* – my stomach!' He closed his eyes.

Beside him, Dr Roger Bryant thought, 'I simply can't decide. This is the most important decision of my life. It could destroy my career . . .'

Armand Dupont shouted excitedly at his son, Jean, 'They are wrong – the Germans, the Americans, the English!' He pulled open an ancient briefcase. 'The decoration on these Kurdish pipes is almost exactly the same as the decoration on the <u>pottery</u> of 5,000 BC.' He waved his arm and almost knocked over the plate that a steward was putting on the table in front of him.

★

On the other side of the plane, Mr Clancy, writer of detective stories, got up from his seat behind Norman Gale, walked to the end of the cabin, and took a European railway timetable from his coat pocket, in order to work out a complicated <u>alibi</u> for one of his characters.

Another passenger, Mr Ryder, was also deep in thought: 'I don't see how I can possibly raise the money for the next payment . . .'

★

Norman Gale got up and went to the toilet. As soon as he had gone, Jane quickly took out a mirror and put on some more lipstick. Then she looked out of the window at the English Channel shining below, as a steward brought her a cup of coffee.

★

A <u>wasp</u> buzzed round Mr Clancy's head, then flew off to investigate the Duponts' coffee cups. Eventually, Jean Dupont managed to kill it, and the cabin was peaceful again.

★

Right at the back of the plane, in seat number two, Madame Giselle's head fell forward. It looked as if she were asleep. But she was not.

Madame Giselle was dead.

Chapter 2 Discovery

Henry Mitchell, the senior steward, walked past the tables in the rear cabin, collecting payment for the food and drinks that had been served to the passengers. The old woman at the back was asleep, and he decided not to wake her up until five minutes before they reached London. When that time arrived, he went and stood beside her. 'Madam, your bill.' He shook her gently by the shoulder and her body slipped down in the seat.

★ ★ ★

Mitchell walked along the rear cabin, asking quietly at each table, 'Excuse me, Sir, are you a doctor?'

Dr Bryant said, 'Yes, *I* am. What's the matter?'

'It's the lady at the end, Sir.'

Dr Bryant got up and went with the senior steward to seat number two. Hercule Poirot, the little man with the moustache, followed them. Bryant bent over the body of the woman. 'She's been dead for at least half an hour,' he said. 'When did you last see her alive?'

'When I brought her coffee, about three-quarters of an hour ago,' said Mitchell.

Their discussion was beginning to cause interest. The other passengers were turning round to listen.

'There is a mark on her neck,' said Monsieur Poirot.

The woman's head had fallen sideways. There was a tiny mark on the side of her neck.

The two Duponts arrived beside them. '*Pardon*. The lady is dead, you say, and there is a mark on her neck?' said Jean. 'There was a wasp flying about.' He showed them the dead insect in his <u>saucer</u>. 'Perhaps she has died of a wasp <u>sting</u>?'

'It is possible,' agreed Dr Bryant. 'Especially if she had a weak heart.'

'Is there anything I should do?' asked Mitchell. 'We'll be landing in London in a minute.'

'There's nothing that can be done. The body must not be moved.'

'*Pardon.* Something has been missed.' Monsieur Poirot pointed at a small yellow and black object lying on the floor.

'Another wasp?' asked the doctor, surprised.

Poirot knelt down and carefully picked up the object. 'It is not a wasp!' He showed them a small <u>dart</u>. It was made from a long <u>thorn</u>, which was <u>stained</u> at its pointed end. Yellow and black silk <u>thread</u> was tied around the top.

'Good gracious me!' Mr Clancy was looking over the steward's shoulder. 'I don't believe it! Gentlemen, this is the type of thorn shot from a <u>blowpipe</u>, the kind that is used by various <u>tribes</u> in South America – and I <u>suspect</u> that on the tip . . .'

'Is the famous <u>arrow</u> poison of the South American Indians,' said Hercule Poirot.

Chapter 3 Croydon Airport

As the plane landed, Mitchell stood in the doorway of the rear cabin. 'I must ask you, Ladies and Gentlemen, to remain in your seats until the police arrive,' he announced.

'Nonsense,' cried Lady Horbury angrily. 'I insist on being allowed to leave at once.'

'I'm sorry, my lady.'

Albert Davis, the second steward, had taken the passengers in the front cabin off the plane through the emergency exit. Then he had gone to call the police. It was not long before a tall police inspector and a uniformed policeman hurried onto the plane. The inspector talked to Mitchell and Dr Bryant, and looked at the dead woman. Then he turned to the passengers. 'Will you please follow me, Ladies and Gentlemen?' he said.

★ ★ ★

Inspector Japp led the passengers to a private room inside the airport. 'If you will remain here, Ladies and Gentlemen, I want to speak to Doctor Bryant. Please come with me, Doctor.'

'May I help?' asked the little man with the moustache.

'Monsieur Poirot!' said the Inspector. 'I didn't recognize you under that blanket. Of course you may join us.'

As the three men left the room, Norman Gale turned to Jane. 'I think I saw you at Le Pinet.'

'Did you?' said Jane.

'I recognized you in the plane. Do you think that woman was really murdered?'

'I suppose so.' Jane shivered. 'It's horrible.'

★ ★ ★

'You turn up in the most unexpected places, Monsieur Poirot,' said Inspector Japp, in a nearby room.

'And why are you here at Croydon airport yourself, my friend?' asked Poirot.

'I'm looking for an international criminal. It's lucky I was here. Now, Doctor, may I have your name and address?'

'Roger James Bryant. 329 Harley Street.'

<u>Constable</u> Rogers, the uniformed policeman, wrote down the information.

'Can you give us any idea of the time of death?'

'The woman had been dead at least half an hour when I examined her. And the steward had spoken to her about an hour before.'

'Did you notice anything strange?'

The doctor shook his head.

'And I was asleep,' said Poirot. He was angry with himself because he had not seen the murder happen. 'I suffer from travel sickness in the air and on the sea. So, I always try to sleep.'

'Any idea about the cause of death, Doctor?'

'I could not say at this stage.'

'Well, I'm afraid you will have to be searched; all the passengers will.'

Dr Bryant smiled. 'In case I have a blowpipe hidden in my luggage, or my pocket?'

Japp nodded to the constable. 'Rogers will do it. By the way, Doctor, do you have any idea what would be likely to be on this . . . ?' Japp pointed to the dart which was lying on the table in front of him.

'Curare is the usual poison used by the people in the tribes, I believe. It is very quick.'

'Is it easy to find?'

'Not for an ordinary person.'

'Then we'll have to search you extra carefully. Rogers!'

The doctor and the constable left the room together.

Japp looked at Poirot. 'A couple of my men are searching the plane. We've got a <u>fingerprint</u> man and a photographer coming along. I think we'd better see the stewards next.' He walked to the door and gave an order. The two stewards came into the room. Davis looked excited. Mitchell was still white and frightened.

'Sit down, Gentlemen,' said Japp. 'Have you brought the passports? Good.' He sorted through them. 'Ah, here we are. Madame Giselle's real name was Marie Morisot. French passport. Do you know anything about her?'

'I've seen her before. She crossed to and from England quite often,' said Mitchell.

'I remember her, too,' said Davis. 'I sometimes saw her on the early service – the eight o'clock from Paris.'

'Which of you was the last to see her alive?'

'I was,' said Mitchell. 'I took her some coffee at about two o'clock.'

'When did you see her next?'

'When I took the bills round, about fifteen minutes later. I thought she was asleep. She must have been dead then!'

'You didn't see this?' Japp pointed to the little dart.

'No, Sir.'

'What about you, Davis?'

'The last time I saw her was when I was handing out the biscuits and cheese. She was all right then.'

'Did this woman speak to anyone on the plane? Did she recognize anyone? asked Japp.

'Not that I saw, Sir,' said Mitchell.

'Davis?'

'No, Sir.'

'Did she leave her seat at all during the journey?'

'I don't think so, Sir.'

'Well, then, that'll be all for now.'

Poirot leaned forward. 'One little question. Did either of you notice a wasp flying about the plane?'

Both men shook their heads.

'*Eh, bien,* it is of no importance,' said Poirot.

As the two stewards left the room, Japp looked through the passports. 'Let's see Lady Horbury first,' he said.

'You will search all the hand luggage of the passengers in the rear cabin very carefully?' asked Poirot.

'Yes, Monsieur Poirot. We must find that blowpipe – if there *is* a blowpipe and we're not all dreaming! Everybody has got to be searched; and every bit of luggage has got to be searched, too.'

'A very *exact* list might be made, perhaps, of everything in these people's possession?'

'If you say so. I don't quite see why, though. We know what we're looking for.'

'I am not so sure. I look for something, but I do not know what it is.'

'You do like to make things difficult, don't you, Monsieur Poirot?'

★

Lady Cicely Horbury told Japp that she was the wife of the Earl of Horbury and that she was returning to London from Le Pinet and Paris. She did not know the dead woman. She had noticed nothing strange during the flight. She was facing towards the front of the plane, and so she could not see anything going on behind her. She thought that two men had left the cabin to go to the toilets, but she was not sure. She had not seen anyone handling anything like a blowpipe. She had not noticed the wasp.

Lady Horbury was followed by the Honourable Venetia Kerr, also returning from the South of France. She had never seen the dead woman before. She had noticed nothing suspicious during the journey. She had seen a wasp annoying some passengers farther down the cabin, soon after lunch was over.

'If you ask me,' said Japp, when Miss Kerr had gone, 'those Frenchmen are the guilty ones. They were just across the aisle from Morisot. Their suitcase is covered with foreign labels. I wouldn't be surprised if they'd been to Borneo or South America, or wherever it is. As for the <u>motive</u>, we can probably get that from Paris. We'll ask the French police – the Sûreté – to help us.'

Poirot smiled. 'It is possible. But, my friend, those two men cannot possibly be murderers! They are famous <u>archaeologists</u>. Monsieur Armand Dupont and his son, Jean. They have just returned from some very interesting archaeological sites in <u>Persia</u>.'

Japp grabbed a passport. 'You're right! Well, let's have a look at them.'

*

Armand Dupont did not know the dead woman. He had noticed nothing on the journey, because he had been talking to his son about the ancient pottery of the Near East. He had not left his seat. Yes, he had seen the wasp towards the end of lunch. His son had killed it.

Jean Dupont confirmed his father's story.

★

Mr Clancy came next. Inspector Japp felt that Mr Clancy knew too much about blowpipes and poisoned darts. 'Have you ever owned a blowpipe yourself?' he asked.

'Well, yes, actually, I have. You see, I was writing a book in which the murder was committed that way, and I needed a drawing to show the position of fingerprints on the blowpipe. I had noticed one in a shop in the Charing Cross Road, in London, so I bought it, and an artist drew it for me – including the fingerprints.'

'Did you keep the blowpipe?'

'Yes.'

'Where is it now?'

'I don't know. I haven't seen it for six months.'

'Did you leave your seat at all in the plane?'

'Yes. I went to get a railway timetable out of my coat pocket. The coat was lying on my suitcase at the back of the cabin.'

'So you passed the dead woman's seat?'

'Yes, but long before anything could have happened. I'd only just drunk my soup.'

Poirot asked about the wasp. Yes, Mr Clancy had noticed a wasp. It had attacked him, just after the steward had brought his coffee. When he tried to hit it, it flew away. Mr Clancy was allowed to leave.

★

Norman Gale was a dentist. He was returning from a holiday at Le Pinet. He had never seen the dead woman, and had noticed nothing suspicious during the journey. He had left his seat once during the journey to go to the toilet. He had not noticed the wasp.

★

James Ryder was returning from a business visit. He did not know the dead woman. Yes, he had the seat in front of her, but he had heard no cry or exclamation. No one had come down the cabin except the stewards. The young Frenchman sitting opposite him had killed a wasp. He had never seen a blowpipe.

★

There was a knock on the door and a police constable came in. 'The sergeant's just found this, Sir.' He laid an object on the table. 'There are no fingerprints.'

It was a native blowpipe.

Japp gasped. 'My goodness! Where was it found?'

'Behind one of the seats, Sir. Number nine.'

'Very entertaining,' said Poirot. 'Number nine was *my* seat.'

Japp smiled at him. 'So, did *you* do it, then, old friend?'

'My friend,' said Poirot seriously, 'when I commit a murder, it will not be with the arrow poison of the South American Indians.'

'Well, it was successful,' said Japp. 'Whoever did it. Only one girl left. Jane Grey. Let's call her in.'

★

Jane Grey worked as a hairdresser in London, and was returning from a holiday in Le Pinet. She had not seen the blowpipe. She did not know the dead woman, but had noticed her at Le Bourget. 'Because she was so very ugly,' she said.

As Jane left, Japp picked up the blowpipe again. 'Where does it come from? We'll have to ask an expert. It may be Malayan or South American or African.'

'Look carefully, my friend,' said Poirot, 'and you will notice the remains of a torn-off price ticket. I think that this pipe was bought in a shop.'

Chapter 4 The _Inquest_

The inquest on Marie Morisot was held four days later. The first witness called was an elderly Frenchman – Maître Alexandre Thibault.

'You have seen the body of the deceased,' asked the coroner. 'Do you recognize it?'

'I do. It is the body of my client, Marie Angélique Morisot.'

'That is the name on her passport. Was she also known by another name?'

'Madame Giselle. She was one of the most famous moneylenders in Paris.'

'Where was her business?'

'Number 3. _Rue Joliette._'

'She travelled to England quite often. Did she also work in this country?'

'Yes. Many of her clients were English.'

'Would she always keep the secret of a client's money problems?'

'Always.'

'Did you know much about her business?'

'No. I was just her lawyer. Madame Giselle ran the business by herself.'

'Was she a rich woman?'

'Very.'

'Did she have any enemies?'

'I don't think so.'

*

'Henry Charles Mitchell. You are the senior steward on the aeroplane _Prometheus_?'

'Yes, Sir.'

'On Tuesday the eighteenth, you were on duty on the 12 o'clock flight from Paris to Croydon. Had you ever seen the deceased before?'

'Yes, Sir. I used to work on the 8.45 a.m. service, and she travelled by that once or twice.'

'Have you ever heard of Madame Giselle?'

'No, Sir.'

The blowpipe was handed to Mitchell. 'Have you ever seen that before?'

'No, Sir.'

★

'Albert Davis. You were working on the *Prometheus* as second steward last Tuesday?'

'Yes, Sir.'

'What was the first that you knew of the <u>tragedy</u>?'

'Mr Mitchell told me that something had happened to one of the passengers.'

'Have you ever seen this before?' The blowpipe was handed to Davis.

'No, Sir.'

★

Dr Bryant gave his name and address and described himself as a specialist in ear and throat diseases.

'Will you tell us, Dr Bryant, exactly what happened on Tuesday the eighteenth?'

'Just before getting into Croydon the chief steward asked if I was a doctor, and told me that one of the passengers was ill. In fact, the woman had been dead for some time.'

'How long, in your opinion?'

'Between thirty minutes and an hour.'

'The cause of death?'

'Impossible to say without a detailed examination.'

'You noticed a small mark on the side of the neck?'

'Yes.'

'Thank you.'

★

'Dr James Whistler. You are a police <u>surgeon</u>?'

'I am.'

'Will you give your <u>evidence</u>?'

'Shortly after three o'clock on Tuesday, I was called to Croydon airport, to inspect the body of a middle-aged woman on the aeroplane *Prometheus*. Death had occurred about an hour before. I noticed a round mark on the side of the neck. This could have been caused by the sting of a wasp or by the dart which was shown to me. The body was taken to the <u>mortuary</u>, where I was able to make a detailed examination. I found that her death was caused by poison. It must have been almost instant.'

'Can you tell us what that poison was?'

'No.'

'Thank you.'

The next person to give evidence was Mr Winterspoon. He was a scientist who worked for the Government, and he knew all about unusual poisons. The coroner held up the dart and asked if he recognized it.

'I do. It was sent to me for <u>analysis</u>. Originally the dart had been dipped in curare – a traditional arrow poison. But more recently it was dipped in the poison of *Dispholidus typus*, or the boomslang.'

'What is a boomslang?'

'A deadly South African tree snake. The poison causes bleeding under the skin and stops the heart.'

★

Detective-Sergeant Wilson described finding the blowpipe behind one of the seats. There were no fingerprints on it. Experiments had also been made with the blowpipe. It was accurate, up to about ten <u>yards</u>.

★

Hercule Poirot had noticed nothing unusual on the journey. He was the person who had found the tiny dart on the floor of the cabin.

★

Neither Lady Horbury nor the Honourable Venetia Kerr had seen anything unusual. They had never seen the deceased before.

★

'You are James Bell Ryder?'

'Yes.'

'What is your profession?'

'I am in charge of the *Ellis Vale Cement Company*.'

'Please examine this blowpipe. Have you ever seen it before?'

'No.'

'You were sitting in seat number four, right in front of the deceased. From that seat you could see almost everyone in the compartment.'

'No. I couldn't see the people on my side. The seats have high backs.'

'But if one of those people had stepped out into the aisle to aim the blowpipe at the deceased, you would have seen them then?'

'Certainly.'

'You didn't see anybody do this?'

'No.'

'Did any of the people in front of you move from their seats?'

'The man two rows in front of me got up and went to the toilet.'

'Was he carrying anything?'

'Nothing.'

'Did anyone else move?'

'The man in front of me came past to the back of the cabin.'

'Did this gentleman have anything in his hands?'

'A pen. When he came back he also had an orange book.'

'Did you leave your seat?'

'Yes, I went to the toilet – and, no, I didn't have a blowpipe in my hand either.'

★

Norman Gale, dentist, and Miss Jane Grey, hairdresser's assistant, were also unable to assist the inquiry. Neither of them had seen anything unusual on the journey.

★

When Mr Clancy was questioned by the coroner, he explained that he had been too busy working out the timetables of foreign train services to notice anything going on around him. The whole cabin might have been shooting poisoned darts out of blowpipes for all he knew.

★

Monsieur Armand Dupont said that he was on his way to London, to give a public talk. He and his son had been having an important conversation, and had not noticed the deceased until her death was discovered.

'Did you know Madame Morisot, or Madame Giselle?'

'No, Monsieur.'

'You have recently returned from the East?'

'From Persia.'

'You and your son have travelled to many foreign parts of the world?'

'Yes.'

'Have you ever come across a tribe of people who use arrows with snake poison on the tips?'

'Never.'

Jean Dupont's evidence was the same as his father's. He had thought it was possible that the deceased had been stung by a wasp, because he had been annoyed by one too, and had finally killed it.

The Duponts were the last witnesses.

* * *

It was an incredible case. A woman had been murdered in mid-air. In front of twelve witnesses, the murderer had placed a blowpipe to his lips and sent the <u>fatal</u> dart through the air and no one had seen the act. It seemed impossible, but the evidence showed that was what had happened. And the murderer must be one of the witnesses themselves.

Because it was still unclear exactly who had committed the murder, the coroner advised the <u>jury</u> to give a <u>verdict</u> of 'murder by a person or persons unknown.' Everyone said they didn't know the dead woman, and there was no obvious motive for the crime. The police would have to find the connection later. The jury must now consider the verdict.

One member of the jury leaned forward. 'Can I ask a question, Sir?' he asked.

'Certainly.'

'You say the blowpipe was found down a seat? Whose seat?'

The coroner looked at his notes. 'The seat was number nine, occupied by Monsieur Hercule Poirot, a well-known private detective who has worked several times in the past with <u>Scotland Yard</u>.'

'And it was Mr Poirot who picked up the dart?'

'Yes.'

The jury left the courtroom to discuss their verdict. They came back after five minutes, and handed a piece of paper to the coroner.

The coroner <u>frowned</u>. 'Nonsense! I can't accept this verdict.'

The jury examined the facts again, and then gave their final verdict.

'Marie Morisot's death was caused by poison. There is no evidence to <u>prove</u> who gave her the poison.'

Chapter 5 After the Inquest

As Jane left the court she found Norman Gale beside her.

'I wonder what was on that paper that the coroner wouldn't accept,' he said.

'I can tell you, I think.' They turned round, to find Monsieur Poirot smiling at them. 'The jury accused me – Hercule Poirot! – of being the murderer. Definitely, I must work to clear my name.' He bowed and walked away.

'Extraordinary little man,' said Gale. 'Now, how about having tea with me?'

'Thank you,' said Jane. 'I would like to.' They found a teashop and sat down at a table.

'It's strange, this murder <u>business</u>,' said Norman, as they waited for a waitress to bring them their tea.

'I know,' said Jane. 'I'm worried about my job. *Antoine's* may not want to employ a girl who's been involved in a murder case. After all, I might actually be the person who murdered her! It wouldn't be very nice having your hair done by someone like that.'

'You're not a murderer! Anyone can see that, just by looking at you,' said Norman.

'I'm not sure,' said Jane. 'I'd like to murder some of my ladies sometimes, if I could be sure no one would find out!'

'Well, you didn't do this particular murder. I'm sure of it!'

'And I know *you* didn't do it. But that won't help if your patients think you did.'

Norman looked thoughtful. 'I hadn't thought of that. A dentist who might be a dangerous killer. It's not a very comfortable idea. I say,' he added, 'you don't mind that I'm a dentist, do you?'

Jane raised her eyebrows. 'Why would I mind?'

'Well, it's not a very romantic profession.'

They both laughed, and then Norman said, 'I feel we're going to be friends. Do you?'

'Yes, I do.'

'Would you have dinner with me one night, and perhaps go to the theatre?'

'Thank you. Yes.'

There was a pause. Then Norman said, 'Jane, who do you think really murdered this Giselle woman?'

'I have no idea. I didn't realise until today that one of the others must have done it.'

'Well, I know I didn't do it, and I know you didn't do it, because I was watching you most of the time.'

'I know you didn't do it, for the same reason. And I know I didn't do it! So it must have been one of the others; but I don't see how we can ever know who it was.'

'Let's think about them all now,' said Norman. 'The stewards?'

'No.'

'I agree. The women opposite us?'

'I don't believe Lady Horbury would go around killing people. And Miss Kerr is far too much of a lady, I'm sure.'

'It can't be Monsieur Poirot, and the doctor doesn't seem likely, either. What about Clancy, who actually confessed to owning a blowpipe?'

'He didn't need to mention it,' Jane pointed out, 'so it looks as though he's all right.'

'Ryder?'

'It might be him.'

'And the two Frenchmen?'

'They're the most likely. They've been to foreign countries, so they could have got the poison there. And they may have had some reason we know nothing about. I thought the younger one looked nice, though; and the father was a sweet man. I hope it isn't them.'

'We don't seem to be making much progress,' sighed Norman.

'I don't see how we can, without knowing a lot of things about the woman. Did she have any enemies, who's going to <u>inherit</u> her money, and all that.'

'There is a good a reason for trying to solve the mystery, you know. Murder doesn't just involve the <u>victim</u> and the killer. It affects other people, too. We're innocent, but this murder has touched us. We don't know how it may change our lives.'

Chapter 6 <u>*Consultation*</u>

Outside the courtroom, Hercule Poirot spoke to Inspector Japp.

'Hello, Poirot,' smiled the inspector. 'You had a lucky escape from being locked up in a police cell.' He introduced a tall, thin man with a sad, clever-looking face. 'This is Monsieur Fournier of the Sûreté. He has come over to England to work with us on this business.'

Fournier bowed and they shook hands.

'I suggest,' said Poirot, 'that you both dine with me, at my apartment. I have also invited Maître Thibault. You see, I wish to prove to you that I am not the murderer.'

'That jury certainly didn't like the look of you,' laughed Inspector Japp.

★ ★ ★

The little Belgian detective provided an excellent meal for his friends. When they had finished eating, the four men began to discuss the mysterious murder.

'Well, said Japp, 'Maître Thibault must go on to another appointment later this evening, so I suggest, to save time, that we start by asking him to tell us all he can about this Giselle woman.'

'In truth,' said the lawyer, 'I know very little about her. Madame Giselle was what you call in this country "a character". She was a pretty young woman, I believe, but then she caught <u>smallpox</u> and lost her good looks. She was a woman who enjoyed power. She was a very clever businesswoman, who never allowed emotions to affect her work. She was known to be completely honest in her work.'

Fournier nodded. 'Yes, she was honest, but according to her personal rules. The police could have caught her – if there had been any evidence of a crime, but . . .' he sighed, sadly, 'nobody would provide the necessary information. It's understandable, when such information would, no doubt, destroy their own <u>reputation</u>.'

'<u>Blackmail</u>?' said Japp.

'Yes. Madame Giselle had her own ways of getting people to pay back the money she lent them. Madame Giselle's clients came from the upper and professional classes. Those people care very much what <u>society</u> thinks of them. They must guard their reputations. It was Madame Giselle's habit before lending money to collect information about her clients, and her intelligence system was an extremely good one. As we said before, according to her own rules Madame Giselle was an honest woman. She protected those clients who kept their promises and paid their <u>debts</u>. I believe that she never used her secret knowledge to obtain money unless that money was owed to her.'

'You mean,' said Poirot, 'that this knowledge was her security?'

'Exactly; and, Gentlemen, her system worked! She very rarely lost her money. A man or woman in an important social position would do anything to get the money to pay her back and prevent a public <u>scandal</u>.'

'And supposing,' said Poirot, 'that there was occasionally a client who couldn't pay – what then?'

'In that case,' said Fournier, 'the information was either published, or was given directly to the person who would be most seriously affected by receiving it.'

'<u>Financially</u>, that did not benefit her?'

'Not directly,' said Fournier.

'But it made the others pay up, eh?' said Japp.

'Exactly.'

Japp rubbed his nose thoughtfully. 'Well, that certainly suggests some possible motives for murder. Who is going to inherit her money?' he asked Thibault.

'She had a daughter,' said the lawyer. 'The girl did not live with her mother – in fact, her mother had not seen her since she was a tiny child; but she made a <u>will</u> many years ago, leaving everything to her daughter, Anne Morisot, except for a small <u>legacy</u> to her maid.'

'Is the <u>fortune</u> large?' asked Poirot.

'I would guess between eight and nine million francs.'

Poirot whistled.

'Why, that must be well over a hundred thousand pounds!' said Japp.

'Mademoiselle Anne Morisot will be a very wealthy young woman,' said Poirot.

'She's lucky that she wasn't on that plane. She might have been suspected of murdering her mother for the money. How old is she now?

'About twenty-four or five,' said the lawyer.

'Well, there's nothing to connect her with the crime. As for this blackmailing business, everyone on that plane denies knowing Madame Giselle. One of them is lying, and we must find out who it is. An examination of her private papers might help, eh, Fournier?'

'My friend,' said the Frenchman, 'as soon as the news came through from Scotland Yard, I went straight to her house. There was a <u>safe</u> there containing papers. All those papers had been burnt.'

'Who by? Why?'

'Madame Giselle's maid, Elise, had orders to open the safe and burn the contents if anything ever happened to her mistress.'

'What?' said Japp.

'You see, Madame Giselle promised her clients that she would deal honestly with them, and she was a woman who kept her promises.'

Japp shook his head.

Maître Thibault rose to his feet. 'Gentlemen, I must go now. If there is any further information I can give you, you know my address.' He shook hands with them and left the apartment.

Chapter 7 Probabilities

'Now,' said Japp, 'there were eleven passengers in the rear cabin of that plane, and two stewards. That's twelve people who could have murdered the old woman. Monsieur Fournier can investigate the French passengers. I'll take the English ones. There are also inquiries to be made in Paris, Fournier.'

'Not only in Paris,' said Fournier. 'In the summer, Giselle did a lot of business at resorts on the coast – Deauville, Le Pinet, Wimereux. She went south, too, to Antibes, Nice, and all those places.'

'Then we must investigate the murder itself, and prove who could possibly have used that blowpipe.' Japp unrolled a large plan of the cabin, and laid it out on the table. 'We can cross

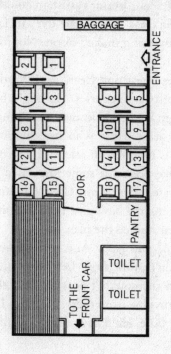

Monsieur Poirot off the list, which brings the number down to eleven. The stewards are unlikely suspects, but they moved around the cabin, and so they could have stood in a place where they could have used that blowpipe – although I don't think that a steward could shoot a poisoned dart out of a blowpipe in a cabin full of people without someone noticing. Of course, the same thing is true for every other person. Whoever did it was extremely lucky!'

'It is, perhaps, a person with a sense of humour,' said Fournier.

'And now we must think about the passengers. Let's start with seat number 16. Jane Grey – she won a lottery prize, and spent the money on a trip to Le Pinet. That means she's a gambler. It's unlikely that she borrowed money from Giselle. And I don't think a hairdresser's assistant could get hold of snake poison. They don't use it as a hair dye. In fact, the murderer made a mistake by using snake poison. Not many people could get hold of it.'

'Which makes one thing clear,' said Poirot. 'The murderer belongs to one of two categories. He might be a man who has travelled to foreign lands, and knows something about poisonous snakes and the native tribes who use the poison to kill their enemies. Or he is involved in scientific research. Winterspoon told me that snake poison is sometimes used in medicine. But neither of those categories fit Jane Grey. A motive seems unlikely. Look, actually using the blowpipe is almost impossible for her.'

The three men studied the plan.

'Here's seat 16,' said Japp. 'And here's Giselle's seat, number two. If Grey didn't move from her seat – and everybody says she didn't – then she couldn't possibly have shot Giselle in the neck with the blowpipe from there. Number 12, opposite, is the dentist, Norman Gale. He'd have a better chance of getting hold of snake poison through his work, or from a scientist friend – but he only left his seat once – to go to the toilet, which is in the opposite direction. And to shoot a blowpipe on his way back that could hit the old lady in the neck, he'd need a magic dart that could turn round the corner. Very unlikely.'

'I agree,' said Fournier.

'We'll cross the aisle now. Number 17.'

'That was my seat originally,' said Poirot. 'I gave it to one of the ladies, who wanted to sit beside her friend.'

'The Honourable Venetia Kerr is very well known in London. She might have borrowed money from Giselle. It doesn't look as though she had any guilty secrets, but maybe she interfered with the results of a horse race or something. If Giselle had turned her head to look out of the window, Venetia Kerr could have shot her diagonally across the cabin, but only if she stood up to do it. She's the sort of woman who goes shooting in the autumn. Shooting a native blowpipe must need similar kinds of skills and she's probably got friends who've been big-game hunting around the world, who could get hold of snake poison for her. What nonsense it all sounds, though!'

'I saw Mademoiselle Kerr at the inquest.' Fournier shook his head. 'It is not easy to connect her with murder.'

'Seat 13,' said Japp. 'Lady Horbury. I wouldn't be surprised if she had a guilty secret or two.'

'She has been losing money at the baccarat table at Le Pinet.'

'Ah. And she's the type of person to be mixed up with Giselle. But how could she have done it? She'd have had to kneel up and lean over the top of her seat, with ten people looking at her!'

'Seats nine and ten,' said Fournier, moving his finger on the plan.

'Hercule Poirot and Dr Bryant,' said Japp. 'Dr Bryant is unlikely to go to a French woman moneylender; but you never know. And he will know medical research people. He could easily have stolen some snake poison while he was visiting a <u>laboratory</u>. But then, why did he mention poison? Why didn't he just say that the woman had died from heart failure?'

'I think that was his first thought,' said Poirot. 'It looked like a natural death, possibly as the result of a wasp sting; there was a wasp, remember?'

'We're not likely to forget. You're always talking about it.'

'However, when I found the poisoned dart on the ground, everything pointed to murder.'

'The dart would have been found anyway.'

Poirot shook his head. 'The murderer could have picked it up secretly.'

'A bit of a risk.'

'You think so now,' said Fournier, 'because you know that it is murder. But when a lady dies suddenly of heart failure, who will notice if a man drops his handkerchief and then picks it up again?'

'True,' agreed Japp. 'Well, Bryant is definitely on the list. He could have leaned round the corner of his seat and blown in the pipe diagonally across the cabin. But nobody saw him!'

'I think there is a reason for that,' said Fournier. 'If you were travelling on a train, and you passed a burning house, everyone would look out of the window at it. At that moment, a man might take out a knife and <u>stab</u> someone, and nobody would see him do it.'

'That is true,' said Poirot. 'And if such a moment occurred during the journey of the *Prometheus*, it would have been created by the murderer.'

'Well, we'll add it to our list of questions,' said Japp. 'Now, seat number eight – Daniel Michael Clancy. A crime writer could easily pretend to have an interest in snake poison and persuade a chemist to show him some. And he was the only passenger to go past Giselle's seat. He could have used that blowpipe without needing the "moment". And he knows all about blowpipes. It looks suspicious to me. Seat number four was Ryder – right in front of Giselle. He went to the toilet, and could have taken a shot at her on the way back. But he'd have been right next to the archaeologists when he did so, and they would have noticed.'

Poirot shook his head. 'You do not know many archaeologists, perhaps? If they were discussing a really important point – *eh bien*, my friend, they would be blind and deaf to whatever was happening around them. They would be living in 5,000 BC. At that moment AD 1935 would not exist for them.'

Japp did not look impressed. 'What can you tell us about the Duponts, Fournier?'

'Armand Dupont is one of the most famous archaeologists in France.'

'That doesn't matter to us. Their position in the cabin is pretty good. And they've travelled to a lot of strange places; they might easily have got hold of snake poison.'

Fournier shook his head. 'The Duponts are devoted to their profession. It is unlikely that they are mixed up in this business.'

'All right. I will find out if Clancy, Bryant and Ryder have ever needed money; if they have seemed worried lately; where they have been during the last year and so on. Wilson can check up on the others. And Monsieur Fournier will investigate the Duponts.'

Fournier nodded. 'I shall return to Paris tonight. There may be more information to find out from Elise, Giselle's maid. And I will check where Giselle had been during the summer. I know she was at Le Pinet once or twice.'

'I would like to go with Monsieur Fournier to Paris,' said Poirot.

Japp looked at Poirot curiously. 'Do you have some ideas?'

'One or two; but it is very difficult. One thing that worries me is the fact that the blowpipe was hidden behind a seat.'

'Whoever did it had to hide the thing somewhere,' said Japp.

'But, my friend, in each window of the plane there is a ventilator, a circle of holes which can be opened or closed by turning a wheel of glass. Those holes are wide enough to push the blowpipe through. What could be simpler than to get rid of it that way?'

'The murderer was afraid of being seen.'

'He was not afraid of someone seeing him put the blowpipe to his lips and sending the fatal dart, but he *was* afraid that they would see him trying to push it through the window?'

'It gives you an idea?' asked Fournier.

'Perhaps . . . Do you have that detailed list of the passengers' belongings that I asked you to get me?'

Chapter 8 The List

'Here you are.' Japp took some pages out of his pocket. Poirot took them and began to read.

James Ryder

Pockets: handkerchief; wallet with seven £1 notes; three business cards; letter from partner George Ebermann hoping that *'the loan has been successfully <u>negotiated</u> . . .'*; cigarette-case; book of matches; keys; French and English coins.
Briefcase: documents about his cement business.

Dr Bryant

Pockets: two handkerchiefs; wallet with £20 and 500 francs; French and English coins; diary; <u>fountain-pen;</u> keys.

Norman Gale

Pockets: handkerchief; wallet with £1 and 600 francs; coins; business cards; *Bryant & May* matchbox – empty; lighter, pipe and tobacco; door key.
Small briefcase: white coat; two dental mirrors; *The Strand Magazine.*

Armand Dupont

Pockets: wallet with £10 and 1000 francs; reading glasses; French coins; cotton handkerchief; cigarettes; book of matches.
Small briefcase: speech to Royal Asiatic Society; two archaeological books; photographs of pottery; pottery pipe stems (Kurdish).

Jean Dupont

Pockets: wallet with £5 and 300 francs; cigarette-case; lighter; two pencils; notebook; French coins.

Daniel Clancy

Pockets: handkerchief; fountain-pen; wallet with £4 and 100 francs; newspaper articles on recent crimes; four pencils; pen-knife; notebook; Italian, French, and English coins; hotel bill – Naples; keys.

Coat pocket: European railway timetable; pair of socks; toothbrush; hotel bill – Paris.

Miss Kerr

Handbag: lipstick; two <u>cigarette-holders</u>; cigarette-case; book of matches; handkerchief; £2; coins; keys.

Small leather case: make-up; manicure set; washing bag containing toiletries: toothbrush, sponge, toothpowder, soap; novel.

Carried *Vogue magazine*.

Miss Grey

Handbag: lipstick; keys; pencil; cigarette case; book of matches; handkerchief; hotel bill – Le Pinet; French phrasebook; purse with 100 francs and French and English coins.

Coat pocket: six postcards of Paris; handkerchief; tube of <u>aspirin</u>.

Lady Horbury

Handbag: two lipsticks; handkerchief; £6; French coins; diamond ring; French stamps; two cigarette-holders; lighter; cigarette-case.

Small leather case: make-up; gold manicure set.

Poirot put the pages down and sighed. 'It is clear to me which person committed the crime. And yet, I cannot see why, or how.'

Japp stared at him. 'Are you saying that by reading this stuff you've got an idea who did it?'

'I think so.'

Japp grabbed the papers and read them through, passing each page to Fournier as he finished it. Then he stared at Poirot. 'Are you joking?'

'No, no.'

Fournier put down the pages. 'I cannot see that this list helps us.'

'Not by itself. But add it to certain facts of the case, no? Well, it may be that I am completely wrong.'

'Well, let's hear your <u>theory</u>, then,' said Japp.

'But, it *is* only a theory. I hoped to find a certain object on that list, and I have found it. But it belongs to the wrong person. Much is not clear to me, but there are some facts which form an obvious pattern. Do you not agree? Well, let us each work to his own idea. I only have a certain suspicion . . .'

Japp rose to his feet. 'I'll work in London, and you will return to Paris, Fournier, with Monsieur Poirot.'

Fournier shook Poirot's hand. 'We will meet at Croydon Airport tomorrow morning, then.'

As the detectives left, Poirot went to a small table and picked up a copy of the *Sketch*. He turned the pages until he found what he was looking for.

'*Two <u>Sun</u> <u>Worshippers</u>,*' said the headline. '*Lady Horbury and Mr Raymond Barraclough at Le Pinet.*' He looked at the two laughing people in bathing-costumes, their arms around each other. 'I wonder . . .' said Hercule Poirot.

Chapter 9 Elise Grandier

As soon as they had arrived in Paris, Poirot and Fournier went to number three, *Rue Joliette*. An old servant let them into the house, unwillingly. 'The police here again! This will give the house a bad name,' he complained.

Madame Giselle's office was a small, windowless apartment on the first floor. There was a safe in one corner, a large desk, and several chairs.

'I will not insult you, my friend, by searching here,' said Poirot. 'If there were anything to find here, you would have found it, I am sure.' He looked across at the safe. 'It was empty?'

'Yes. The maid destroyed everything.'

'Ah, yes, the maid. There is no personal touch in this room . . . I find that interesting. Come on, let us see this maid.'

* * *

Elise Grandier was a middle-aged woman with a red face and small, intelligent eyes.

'Mademoiselle Grandier,' said Fournier, 'Monsieur Poirot and I have returned today from London. The inquiry into the death of Madame took place yesterday. Madame was poisoned.'

The Frenchwoman shook her head. 'Poisoned? Who could have done such a thing?'

'Perhaps you can help us find out, Mademoiselle?'

'I will do all I can to help the police, Monsieur. But I know nothing at all.'

'You know that Madame had enemies?'

'That is not true. Why should she?'

'Come, Mademoiselle,' said Fournier. 'Being a moneylender can sometimes be . . . unpleasant.'

'It is true that sometimes Madame's clients were not reasonable,' agreed Elise.

'They made scenes, eh? Threatened her?'

The maid shook her head. 'No, no. They did not threaten. They cried, complained, swore that they could not pay her.' She shrugged her shoulders. 'They usually paid in the end.'

'Madame Giselle was a hard woman. You don't feel sorry for the victims?'

'Victims! Is it necessary to get into debt, to borrow money and then expect to keep it as a gift? It is not! Madame lent, and she expected repayment. That is fair. She had no debts. You say that Madame was a hard woman, but it is not the truth! Madame was kind. She gave money to charities. You do not understand Madame at all!'

'You said that Madame's clients usually paid in the end. Do you know how she made them pay?'

'I know nothing, Monsieur.'

'You knew enough to burn Madame's papers.'

'I was following her instructions. If she died away from home, I was to destroy her business papers.'

'The papers in the safe downstairs?' asked Poirot.

'That is right.'

Poirot smiled. 'But the papers were not in the safe, were they? That safe is too old-fashioned. Anyone could open it. The papers were kept elsewhere – in Madame's bedroom, perhaps?'

Elise paused a moment and then answered. 'Yes. Madame pretended to clients that papers were kept in the safe, but in reality, everything was in Madame's bedroom.'

'Will you show us?'

★ ★ ★

The two men followed Elise to the bedroom, where she lifted the lid of a chest. 'The papers were in here, Monsieur. They were kept in a large sealed envelope.'

'You told me nothing of this,' said Fournier, 'when I questioned you three days ago.'

'You asked me where the papers were that should be in the safe, Monsieur. I told you I had burned them. That was true. Exactly where the papers were kept seemed unimportant.'

'Those papers should not have been burnt.'

'I obeyed Madame's orders.'

'You did what you thought was right, I know,' said Fournier soothingly. 'Now, listen carefully, Mademoiselle. Madame was murdered, possibly by someone whom she had dangerous information about. That information was in those papers you burnt. It is possible that you read those papers before putting them into the fire. No one will blame you for doing this. In fact, any information you have learned may help the police to bring the murderer to justice. Therefore, Mademoiselle, answer truthfully. Did you read those papers?'

'No, Monsieur. I burnt the envelope without opening it.'

Chapter 10 The Little Black Book

Fournier could see that she was speaking the truth. 'It is a pity.' He sat down and took a notebook from his pocket. 'Mademoiselle, did you ever see the clients who came to the house?'

'Almost never. They came at night.'

'Had Madame Giselle been in Paris before her journey to England?'

'She returned to Paris the afternoon before. She had been to Deauville, Le Pinet, and Paris–Plage. She was happy. Her trip had been profitable. She asked me to call *Universal Airlines* and book a flight to England for the following day. The early morning flight was full, but she got a seat on the 12 o'clock flight.'

'Did any clients come to see Madame that evening?'

'I am not sure. Georges, the doorman, would know.'

Fournier took some press photographs from his pocket of various witnesses leaving the coroner's court. 'Do you recognize any of these people, Mademoiselle?'

Elise gazed at each one in turn. 'No, Monsieur.'

'We must try Georges then.' Fournier rose to his feet. 'Come, Monsieur Poirot. Oh, I'm sorry. You are looking for something?'

Poirot was wandering round the room. 'It is true. I am looking for something I do not see – photographs of Madame Giselle's family.'

Elise shook her head. 'She had no family.'

'She had a daughter,' said Poirot <u>sharply</u>.

'That is so, Monsieur, but it was long ago. And Madame had not seen her since she was a baby.'

'But she left her money to this daughter, didn't she?'

'<u>Blood is thicker than water</u>.'

'She left you a legacy. Did you know that?'

'Yes. I am very grateful.'

'Well,' said Fournier, 'we'll go now. On the way out I'll have a word with old Georges.'

'I will follow you in a minute, my friend,' said Poirot.

Fournier left and Poirot sat down and stared at Elise. 'Mademoiselle Grandier, do you know who murdered your mistress?'

'No, Monsieur. I swear it.'

Poirot looked at her carefully, then nodded. 'I believe you. Have you any idea who might have done such a thing?'

'No, Monsieur.'

Poirot leaned forward. 'Mademoiselle Grandier, it is my job to believe nothing I am told – nothing that is not proved. And so, I suspect anybody connected with a crime, until that person is proved innocent.'

'You suspect *me* of having murdered Madame? That is a terrible thought!'

'No, Elise. Madame's killer was a passenger in the aeroplane. But you might have helped with the murder. You might perhaps have given someone the details of Madame's journey.'

'I did not! I swear it!'

Poirot looked at her in silence. Then he nodded his head. 'But there is something that you are hiding. I know. Will you not tell me what it is?'

Elise hesitated. 'Madame trusted me. I have always carried out her orders faithfully.'

'You were grateful for something she had done for you?'

'Yes, Monsieur. I was <u>involved with</u> a man – and I had a child. Madame arranged for the baby to be brought up by some good people on a farm. It was then that she told me that she was also a mother.'

'Did she tell you the age of her child, or where it was?'

'No, Monsieur. She said that the girl would be taught a trade or profession, and would inherit her money when she died.'

'She told you nothing about the father?'

'No, but I think the father of the child was an Englishman.'

'Why?'

'There was a bitterness in Madame's voice when she spoke of the English. It is only an idea.'

'A very valuable one.' There was a pause. 'And now, Mademoiselle Elise, what is this something that you have not mentioned?'

Elise left the room, and returned a few minutes later carrying a small black notebook. 'This book went everywhere with Madame. When she was about to leave for England, she could not find it. After she had gone I found it under the bed. I burned the papers as soon as I heard of Madame's death, but I did not burn the book. She left no instructions about that.'

'When the police came to examine her rooms, they found the safe empty. You told them that you had burnt the papers, but actually you did not burn the papers until afterwards.'

'It is true, Monsieur. Whilst they were looking in the safe I removed the papers from the chest. I burnt them as soon as I could. I had to carry out Madame's orders. You will not tell the police? It might be a serious matter for me.'

'I see no need to tell Monsieur Fournier the exact time, Mademoiselle. Now let me see if there is anything useful in this little book.' He took the book from the maid and turned the pages. Each entry was a number, followed by a short description, such as:

CX 256. Colonel's wife. Stationed Syria. Stolen money.
GF 342. French Deputy. Stavisky connection.

'This may be very valuable, Mademoiselle. You were right to give it to me. You will not be blamed for not giving it to the police sooner.' He got up. 'One last question. Who did you call to reserve a seat in the aeroplane for Madame Giselle?'

'I rang up the company office of *Universal Airlines*, Monsieur.'

'In the *Boulevard des Capucines*?'

'That's right. 254 *Boulevard des Capucines*.'

Poirot wrote down the address, and left the room.

Chapter 11 The American

Fournier was talking to old Georges. The detective looked annoyed.

'Just like the police,' the old man complained. 'Asking the same questions over and over again. I have been telling you the truth. Yes, a woman did come to see Madame the night before she left for England. I did not recognize her. There! I have explained it clearly four or five times.'

'You cannot remember if she was tall or short, dark or fair, young or old? That is hard to believe.'

'What do I care? I am ashamed to be mixed up with the police!'

Poirot slipped his arm through Fournier's. 'Come, my friend. Let us go and eat.' He smiled at the old man. 'The lady was neither tall nor short, fair nor dark, thin nor fat. But this you can tell us: was she a lady of fashion?'

'A lady of fashion?' Georges was surprised.

'I am answered,' said Poirot. 'She was. And I have an idea that she would look good in a bathing-costume. Do you not agree? See here.' He showed the old man a page torn from the *Sketch*. A small flash of recognition showed in the doorman's eyes. There was a moment's pause. 'Do you not agree?'

'They look good enough, those two,' said the old man, handing the page back. 'To wear nothing at all would be nearly the same thing.' He laughed as Poirot and Fournier stepped out into the sunlit street.

★ ★ ★

Over lunch, Poirot took out Giselle's notebook. Fournier was very excited. He turned the pages, and wrote in his own notebook. Then he looked across at Poirot. 'Have you read this?'

45

'I have only glanced at it. May I?' Poirot took the book and began to read. He put it down as the cheese plate arrived.

'There are certain interesting entries,' began Fournier.

'Five,' said Poirot.

'I agree.' Fournier read them out from his notebook:

'*CL 52. English Lady. Husband.*

RT 362. Doctor. Harley Street.'

'Ah! That is where the doctors who look after the rich people in London have their offices, is it not?' He returned to the list.

'*MR 24. Fake Antiques.*

XVB 724. English. Stealing from company.

GF 45. Attempted Murder. English.'

'Excellent, my friend,' said Poirot. 'Of all the notes in that book, those five seem to be the only ones connected to the passengers on that aeroplane. Let us think about them one by one.'

'*English Lady. Husband,*' said Fournier. 'Lady Horbury is a serious gambler. It is likely that she would borrow money from Giselle. The word *husband* may either mean that Giselle expected the husband to pay his wife's debts, or that she had a secret of Lady Horbury's, which she threatened to tell her husband.'

'I think it is the second one myself,' said Poirot. 'And that the woman who visited Giselle the night before the journey was Lady Horbury. The doorman is protecting her. He said he could not remember the visitor, but he reacted, very slightly, when I showed him a picture of her from the *Sketch*.'

'She followed Giselle to Paris from Le Pinet. It looks as though she was quite desperate.'

'I think that may be true.'

'But it does not fit with your theory, eh?'

'I have the right clue pointing to the wrong person.'

'Would you tell me what it is?' asked Fournier.

'No, because I may be wrong. And that might confuse you. No, let us each work according to our own ideas. To continue with the little book.'

'*RT 362. Doctor. Harley Street,*' read out Fournier.

'Dr Bryant, perhaps?'

'*MR 24. Fake Antiques* might be the Duponts, but I can't believe it. Monsieur Dupont is a world-famous archaeologist, with a reputation for being honest. Then there is: *XVB 724. English. Stealing from company.*'

'Who steals from his employer?' asked Poirot. 'A lawyer? A bank clerk? A businessman? Mr James Ryder is our only businessman. He may have stolen money from his company, and he may have borrowed from Giselle to stop his theft from being noticed. And the last entry: *GF 45. Attempted Murder. English* – this gives us a very wide field. Author, dentist, doctor, businessman, steward, hairdresser's assistant, aristocrat. And so, where next, my friend?'

'To the Sûreté. They may have some news for me.'

'I will come with you. And then I have a little investigation of my own to make. Perhaps, you will help me?'

★ ★ ★

At the Sûreté, Poirot saw the Chief of the Detective Force, whom he had met some years ago on a case. Monsieur Gilles was friendly and polite. 'I am happy to learn that you are investigating this case, Monsieur Poirot. Madame Giselle was very well known in Paris. And the manner of her death – extraordinary! A poisoned dart from a blowpipe in an aeroplane. Is it possible that such a thing could happen?'

'That is my point exactly!' cried Poirot. 'Ah, here is Fournier. With news, I see.'

Fournier was excited. 'A Greek antique dealer, Zeropoulos, has a shop in the *Rue S. Honoré*. He says he sold a blowpipe and darts, three days before the murder. We must interview him.'

★ ★ ★

Monsieur Zeropoulos was delighted to see the police. Yes, he had sold a South American blowpipe and darts. 'I sell a little of everything, Gentlemen! Persia is my speciality. Monsieur Dupont himself comes often to see what new items I have for sale, and to give me his opinion. But as well as my valuable collection, which the experts respect, I also sell cheap foreign rubbish – from the South Seas, India, Japan, Borneo. The blowpipe was in that tray there, with a shell necklace and some green beads. Nobody noticed it until this American comes in and asks me what it is.'

'An American?' said Fournier.

'Exactly. I tell him about the deadly poisons used by certain native tribes. I explain how unusual it is that I have anything like this to sell. I tell him my price and he pays. I give him the blowpipe and the darts and it is finished. But when I read of this incredible murder, I wonder. And so I call the police.'

'This blowpipe and dart,' said Fournier, 'could you identify them? They are in London now, but you will get a chance to look at them.'

'The blowpipe was this long,' Monsieur Zeropoulos measured a space on his desk, 'and this thick, like this pen of mine. It was light in colour. The darts were long and pointed, dark at the tips, tied with red silk.'

'*Red* silk?' asked Poirot.

'Yes, Monsieur.'

Poirot gave a satisfied smile.

'Can you describe this American?' asked Fournier.

Zeropoulos raised his hands. 'His voice was <u>nasal</u>. He could not speak French. He was chewing gum. He had on glasses with dark frames. He was tall and not very old. He wore a hat. He was not remarkable in any way.'

★ ★ ★

'And now, my friend,' said Poirot, as they left the shop, 'come with me to the *Boulevard des Capucines*.'

'That is . . .?'

'The office of *Universal Airlines*.'

'But we have already talked to them. They could tell us nothing of interest.'

'Ah, but you did not know what questions to ask.'

★ ★ ★

In the office of *Universal Airlines*, Jules Perrot said he was happy to help the police if he could.

'It is about the murder of Madame Giselle,' explained Poirot.

'Ah, yes. I have already answered some questions on the subject.'

'But it is necessary to have the facts exactly. Now, Madame Giselle booked her seat, when?'

'By telephone, on the 17th.'

'For the 12 o'clock service on the following day?'

'Yes, Monsieur.'

'But I understand that Madame wished for a seat on the 8.45 a.m. service?'

'Madame's maid asked for the 8.45 service, but that service was booked up, so we gave her a seat on the 12 o'clock instead.'

'I see. But that is strange. Because a friend of mine went to England on the 8.45 flight that morning, and the plane was half empty.'

Fournier looked at Poirot in surprise, but said nothing.

'Ah, well, sometimes people do not arrive at the last minute, and so there are empty seats . . . sometimes there are mistakes. The people at Le Bourget are not always accurate . . .' A drop of sweat appeared on Perrot's forehead.

'Two possible explanations,' said Poirot, 'but not true. This is a case of murder, Monsieur Perrot. If you keep back any information, it may be very serious for you.'

Perrot began to shake.

'Come,' said Poirot. 'How much were you paid, and who paid you?'

'F–five thousand francs. I had no idea . . . I meant no harm . . . A man came in. He said he wanted to get a <u>loan</u> from Madame Giselle, but he needed their meeting to be accidental. He said it would give him a better chance. He knew she was flying to England on the following day. He asked me to tell her that the early service was full and book her seat number two in the *Prometheus*. I saw nothing wrong. Americans do business in unusual ways . . .'

'Americans?' asked Fournier.

'Yes, he was an American.'

'Describe him.'

'Tall, with grey hair and dark–framed glasses.'

'Did he book a seat himself?'

'Yes, Monsieur, seat number one. Next to Madame Giselle.'

'In what name?'

'Silas Harper.'

'There was no one of that name travelling, and no one sat in number one.' Poirot shook his head gently.

'I saw in the paper that there was no one of that name, and so I thought there was no need to mention the matter. Since this man did not go by the plane . . .'

Fournier looked at Perrot coldly. 'You have hidden important facts from the police. This is a very serious matter.'

★ ★ ★

On the pavement outside the office, Fournier removed his hat and bowed. 'Congratulations, Monsieur Poirot. What gave you this idea?'

'On our flight over from England this morning, I heard a man saying that he had crossed on the morning of the murder in a nearly empty plane. And then Elise said that she rang up the office of *Universal Airlines* and that there was no room on the early morning flight. Those two statements did not match. The steward on the *Prometheus* had seen Madame Giselle before on the early service, so it was clearly her habit to go by the 8.45 a.m. plane. But somebody wanted her to go on the 12 o'clock. Why did the office tell Elise that the early flight was full? A mistake, or a deliberate lie? I thought it was a lie, and I was right.'

'Every minute this case gets more puzzling. First we seem to be looking for a woman. Now it is an American man.'

Poirot nodded gently. 'It is easy to be an American, here in Paris! The nasal voice, the chewing gum, the glasses, they all belong to the stage American . . .'

He took from his pocket the page he had torn from the *Sketch*, and stared at it.

Chapter 12 At Horbury Chase

Lord Stephen Horbury got up from the breakfast table, left the dining-room, and went upstairs. He was twenty-seven years old, and looked like a typical sportsman. He was also kind-hearted, loyal and very determined.

He knocked on a door and a clear voice cried, 'Come in.'

Lord Horbury walked into his wife's bedroom. She was sitting up in bed, opening her letters. Three years ago, her breathtaking beauty had driven him mad with love. Now, he was mad no longer.

'Stephen?' she said, surprised.

'Why are you here, Cicely?'

Lady Horbury shrugged her beautiful shoulders. 'Why not?'

'We agreed to stop living together. You have the town house and a generous allowance. As long as you behave yourself, you can go your own way. Why have you come back so suddenly? It's money, I suppose?'

'How I hate you. You're the <u>meanest</u> man alive. You advertised in the newspapers that you would no longer pay my debts. Was that a gentlemanly thing to do?'

'I warned you. Twice, I paid, but there are limits. It's because you've spent so much of my money that there's a <u>mortgage</u> on my family's land.'

'The land! That's all you care about! Hunting and shooting and boring old farmers. God, what a life for a woman.'

'Some women enjoy it.'

'Women like Venetia Kerr. Well, she's half a horse herself! You should have married her!'

Lord Horbury walked over to the window. 'I married you,' he said, quietly.

'And you can't get rid of me!' Cicely laughed.

'So, tell me, why have you come here? You hate the place.'

'I thought it better, just now.'

'Just now?' He repeated the words thoughtfully. 'Cicely, did you borrow from that French moneylender? The woman who was murdered on your plane back from Paris?'

'Of course not!'

'Cicely, the police of two countries are working on that murder. If you did do business with this Giselle, they will find out. We must be prepared. You must think of your position.'

Cicely sat up angrily in bed. 'Why are you so worried about me? You don't care what happens to me. You hate me. You'd be glad if I died tomorrow!'

'I care about my family name – an old-fashioned idea which you probably think is <u>ridiculous</u>. But there it is.'

Stephen turned away from her and left the room.

Chapter 13 At Antoine's Hairdressing Salon

Jane arrived at work on the morning after the inquest, to find that her first customer of the day was waiting for her. The woman was looking into the mirror and saying to a friend, 'Darling, my face looks awful this morning.'

'It looks the same as usual to me, my sweet,' replied the friend. As Jane arrived, the friend turned to stare at her. Then she said, 'It *is*, darling! I'm *sure* of it.'

'Good morning, Madam,' said Jane. 'It's a long time since we've seen you here. Have you been abroad?'

'Antibes.' The customer was also staring at Jane. 'Tell me, are you the girl who gave evidence at the inquest yesterday? The girl in the aeroplane?'

'Yes, Madam.'

'How exciting! Do tell me about it.'

Jane had no choice but to answer their questions. What had the old woman looked like? Was Lady Horbury really on board? Who did Jane think had actually committed the murder? And so on and so on.

It was the first of many similar conversations. By the end of the week Jane felt that if she had to go through the story once more, she would scream or attack her next customer with the hairdryer. Instead, she went to ask Monsieur Antoine for a pay rise.

'How dare you ask that, when you have been mixed up in a murder case?' he demanded, angrily. 'Many employers would have dismissed you immediately.'

'Nonsense,' said Jane. 'People are coming here because of me. If you want me to leave, I'll go and get what I want from *Henri's* or the *Maison Richet*.'

Monsieur Antoine agreed, unwillingly, to Jane's demands.

* * *

Jane decided to celebrate her pay rise that Saturday by buying herself lunch at the *Corner House* café and listening to music while she ate.

She sat down at a table where a middle-aged woman and a young man were already sitting. The woman finished her lunch, and called for her bill. Then she picked up her parcels and left. As usual, Jane read a book while she ate. Looking up as she turned a page, she saw the young man sitting opposite staring at her. His attractive face seemed familiar.

'You do not recognize me, Mademoiselle?' he asked. 'We have not been introduced, it is true. Unless you call murder an introduction, and the fact that we both gave evidence in court.'

'Of course!' said Jane. 'You are . . . ?'

'Jean Dupont.' He seemed very pleased to see her. 'My father has been to Edinburgh to give a talk. Tomorrow we return to France.'

'I see.'

'The police have not made an <u>arrest</u> yet?'

'No. There has been no more news about it in the papers. Maybe they've given up. Who do you think did it?' asked Jane.

Jean shrugged. 'Well, it wasn't me. The woman was far too ugly!'

'Wouldn't you rather kill an ugly woman than a pretty one?'

He laughed. 'No, no! If a good-looking woman behaves badly towards you, you say, "Good, I will kill her. It will be most satisfying". But an ugly old woman – why bother to kill her?'

'Well, that's one way of looking at it.' Jane frowned. 'But perhaps she was young and pretty once?'

'It is the great tragedy of life, that we must all grow old.'

'You're an archaeologist, aren't you?' she asked 'You dig things up?'

Jean Dupont happily began to talk about his work, and she listened with great interest.

'You've been to so many countries,' she sighed at last. 'You've seen so much. It sounds fascinating. I will never go anywhere or see anything.'

'You would like to go abroad? To see wild parts of the earth? There are no hairdressing salons in the jungle, you know!'

Jane laughed.

'Mademoiselle,' Jean said, a little embarrassed, 'as I am returning to France tomorrow, would you have dinner with me tonight?'

'I'm so sorry, I can't. I'm having dinner with someone else.' In fact, she was meeting Norman Gale.

'Ah! And I do not know when I shall be in London again! It is sad! I hope I shall see you again, very much,' he said, and sounded as though he meant it.

Chapter 14 The Shadow of Suspicion

'There, that's over,' said Norman Gale, as he finished filling the woman's tooth. 'And you'll come back next Tuesday, so I can do the other fillings?'

His patient explained that she was going abroad suddenly, and must cancel her next appointment. She would let him know when she got back. Then she hurried out of the <u>surgery</u>.

'Well,' said Gale, 'that's all for today.'

'Lady Higginson rang up to cancel her appointment next week,' said Nurse Ross. 'And Colonel Blunt can't come on Thursday.'

Every day it was the same. Cancelled appointments. Excuses. *"I've got a cold." "I'm going away."* Norman had seen the panic in his last patient's eye as he reached for the <u>drill</u>. He could hear her thinking; *'He was in that aeroplane when that woman was murdered . . . You do hear of people going mad and committing crimes for no particular reason. It isn't safe. Murderers look the same as other people, I've heard . . .'*

'I'm afraid it will be quiet next week, Miss Ross,' he sighed.

'Well, you need a rest. You've been working so hard.'

The telephone rang and she left the room to answer it.

Norman began to clean his medical equipment. 'It's funny,' he thought. 'Murder affects all sorts of things you'd never think of . . . What would happen if they arrested Lady Horbury? Would my patients come back? Oh, I don't care. Yes, I do, because of Jane. She's so lovely. And I can't have her – yet.' He smiled. 'She cares about me, though. She'll wait. <u>Damn it</u>, I *will* go to Canada – yes, and I'll make money there.'

Nurse Ross returned. 'Mrs Lorrie . . .'

' . . . is going to Timbuktu,' laughed Norman, bitterly. 'You'd better look for another job, Nurse Ross. If the murderer isn't found soon, this dental practice is finished.'

★ ★ ★

That evening, as Jane had dinner with Norman, she noticed the worried expression on his face. 'Norman, are things going badly?' she asked, at last.

'It's a bad time of year.'

'Don't be silly! I can see that you're worried to death!'

'I'm not. I'm just annoyed.'

'Are people scared . . .'

' . . . of having their teeth fixed by a possible murderer? Yes.'

'How unfair!'

'It is, isn't it?'

'Somebody ought to do something.'

'I'd like to. If I was a young man in a book, I'd follow someone until I found a clue.'

Suddenly, Jane pulled his sleeve. 'Look, there's Mr Clancy – you know, the crime author – sitting over there by himself. He was on the plane. If you want to follow someone, why don't we follow him? You never know. We might discover something.'

★ ★ ★

When Mr Clancy went out into Dean Street, Norman and Jane were close behind him. He walked quickly, and it was not clear where he was going. He seemed to be wandering about in circles.

'He's afraid that someone might be following him,' whispered Jane. 'He's trying to confuse them.'

They turned a corner and discovered Mr Clancy standing in front of a butcher's shop. The shop was shut, but something seemed to have caught his attention.

'Perfect,' he said aloud. He took out a notebook and wrote something down. Then he walked off towards the nearby streets of Bloomsbury.

As he stopped by some traffic lights and waited to cross a busy road, Norman and Jane came up beside him. He was talking to himself, and they heard him saying; *'Why* doesn't she speak? There *must* be a reason . . .' The lights went green, and they all crossed the road together. As they reached the opposite pavement he said, 'Of course! *That's* why she's got to be silenced!'

He walked on, and they continued to follow him, until suddenly, he stopped at a house, opened the front door and went in.

'It's his own house,' said Norman, disappointed. '47 Cardington Square. The address he gave at the inquest.'

'Oh, well,' sighed Jane, 'perhaps he'll come out again. Anyway, we have heard something. A woman is going to be silenced!'

A voice came out of the darkness. 'Good evening.' A magnificent moustache appeared. 'A fine night for hunting, is it not?' said Hercule Poirot.

Chapter 15 In Bloomsbury

'Monsieur Poirot!' said Norman Gale. 'Are you still trying to prove your innocence?'

'Ah, so you remember our conversation? And you suspect poor Mr Clancy?'

'So do you,' said Jane, 'or you wouldn't be here.'

He looked at her thoughtfully. 'What would you say the most important thing was to consider when you are trying to solve a murder, Mademoiselle?'

'Finding the murderer,' said Jane.

'Justice,' said Norman.

Poirot shook his head. 'There are more important things than finding the murderer. And it is sometimes difficult to say exactly what one means by justice. I believe the important thing is to clear the innocent of any blame. Because until one person is proved guilty, everyone else connected with the crime will suffer.'

'How true that is,' said Norman.

Jane said, 'We both know it!'

Poirot looked at them. 'I see you have been finding that out for yourselves. Now, as we are looking for the same answers, let us join together. I am going to visit Mr Clancy. I suggest that Mademoiselle comes with me. She can pretend to be my secretary. Here, Mademoiselle, is a notebook and a pencil. We shall meet Mr Gale in an hour's time, at the restaurant *Monseigneur's*. We will compare notes then.'

'Right,' said Norman.

Poirot walked up to the door and rang the bell. Jane followed him nervously, holding the notebook. The door was opened by an elderly woman, dressed in black.

Poirot said, 'Mr Clancy?'

The woman beckoned them inside. 'What name, Sir?'

'Hercule Poirot.'

She led them upstairs into a room on the first floor. 'Mr Air Kule Pwo Row,' she announced.

The room was very untidy. The floor was covered with piles of paper, cardboard files, bottles of beer, books, cushions, cups and plates, and a large number of fountain-pens. In the middle of the mess, Mr Clancy was trying to put a roll of film into a camera. He looked up at his visitors and put down the camera. Then he came forward to shake Poirot's hand. 'I'm very glad to see you!'

'You remember me, I hope?' said Poirot. 'And my secretary, Miss Grey? We were also passengers on the aeroplane from Paris on that terrible day.'

'How d' you do, Miss Grey.' Mr Clancy shook hands. 'Of course I remember you, Monsieur Poirot! I didn't know Miss Grey was your secretary. I thought she worked in a hairdressing salon?'

'As my secretary, Miss Grey sometimes has to take on undercover work – you understand? Secret work.'

'Of course! I forgot you're a private detective. Do sit down, Miss Grey. No, not there – I think there's orange juice on that chair. And you sit here, Monsieur Poirot. Would you like some beer?'

'Thank you, no.'

Mr Clancy sat down himself, and looked at Poirot. 'You've come to talk about the murder of Giselle. An amazing case. A blowpipe in an aeroplane. An idea I have used myself, as I told you. It was a shocking event, but I must say, Monsieur Poirot, that I found it rather exciting.'

'The crime interested you professionally, Mr Clancy?'

'Exactly! And you would think that the police would understand that! But no, when I try to help them solve the case by describing my own blowpipe, they decide to suspect *me*!'

'It does not seem to affect you very much,' smiled Poirot.

'Ah, but you see,' Mr Clancy leaned forward, 'I'm putting Inspector Japp into my next book.'

'You are lucky, Monsieur,' said Poirot. 'As a writer you have the power of the pen over your enemies.'

'I'm writing a story about this murder. I shall call it *The Air Mail Mystery*, and I shall include all the real passengers as characters. I believe it will be a great success.'

'Won't you get into trouble?' asked Jane.

Mr Clancy turned to her. 'No, no, dear lady. If I were to make one of the passengers the murderer, well, yes, they could probably fight me in the law courts. But I have a completely unexpected solution in the last chapter. A girl gets into the plane at Le Bourget and hides under Madame Giselle's seat. She has with her a tube of gas. She opens it and everybody becomes <u>unconscious</u> for three minutes. She comes out from under the seat, fires the poisoned dart, and jumps out of the plane with a <u>parachute</u>.'

'Why doesn't she become unconscious from the gas too?' asked Jane.

'She's wearing a gas mask,' said Mr Clancy.

'And she lands in the sea?'

'No, on the French coast.'

'But nobody could hide under a seat; there wouldn't be room.'

'There will be room in my aeroplane!'

'And the motive of the lady?' asked Poirot.

'I haven't decided. Probably Giselle was blackmailing the girl's lover, and so he killed himself. She wants <u>revenge</u>.'

'And how did she get hold of the poison?'

'That's the really clever part,' said Mr Clancy. 'The girl's a snake charmer and she gets the poison from one of her snakes.'

'But, good Heavens!' said Hercule Poirot. 'What drama!'

'You can't be too dramatic,' said Mr Clancy. 'After all, you don't want a detective story to be like real life. The murders in the papers are so boring.'

'Come, Monsieur, would you say that our little murder is boring?'

'Well, no. In fact, sometimes, I can't believe it really happened.'

'Monsieur Clancy,' said Poirot, 'you are a very clever man. The police have not asked your advice. But I would like to.'

Mr Clancy's face went pink with pleasure. 'That's very nice of you!'

'I would be most interested to know who you believe committed the crime. If you had to make a guess, who would you choose?'

'Oh, one of the two Frenchmen, I suppose. She was French, after all, and they were sitting quite close to her.'

'It depends so much on motive,' said Poirot thoughtfully.

'And I believe that's a little difficult in this case. There's a daughter who inherits a fortune, I've heard. But anyone on board who owed Madame Giselle money would also benefit, because now they won't have to pay it back.'

'True. And there are other possibilities. What if Madame Giselle knew of something – attempted murder, shall we say – by one of those people?'

'Attempted murder?' said Mr Clancy. 'That's a very strange idea.'

'In cases like this, one must think of everything.'

'Ah! But it's no good thinking. You've got to *know*.'

'You are very right. Now, this blowpipe – you bought it, you say, at a shop in the Charing Cross Road? Can you remember the name of that shop? I ask because I wish to buy one and make a little experiment.'

'Well, it might have been *Absolom's*, or *Mitchell & Smith*. I don't know. But you may not find one. They don't keep sets of them, you know.'

'I can try. Miss Grey, would you kindly write down those names?'

Jane opened her book and made a note of them.

'And now,' said Poirot, 'I have taken up enough of your time. I will leave, with a thousand thanks for your assistance.'

'Not at all, not at all,' said Mr Clancy. 'In fact, I'm feeling very happy tonight. I was having trouble with a short story I was writing – I couldn't get the ending right, and I also needed a good name for the criminal. Well, I've just seen the name I want over a butcher's shop. *Pargiter*. That sounds exactly right. And five minutes later I solved my other problem. Why won't the girl speak? The hero of the story tries to make her talk, but she refuses. There's never any real reason, of course, why she shouldn't tell him everything immediately, but you have to try to think of something that's not too silly. And it has to be something different in every book.' He smiled gently at Jane. 'It is sometimes very hard to be an author!'

Chapter 16 Poirot Sets a Trap

Norman Gale was waiting for Poirot and Jane at the restaurant. 'Well?' he asked, when they had chosen their food from the menu, 'How did you get on?'

'Miss Grey,' said Poirot, 'has proved herself to be the super-secretary.'

'I didn't do much,' said Jane. 'Did you really want those addresses?'

'They might be useful. Although the blowpipe found in the plane was bought in Paris by an American gentleman.'

'But there wasn't an American gentleman in the aeroplane!' said Jane.

Poirot smiled. 'Exactly. We now have an American, just to make it more difficult!'

'Well it wasn't Mr Clancy. He'd got one blowpipe already, so he wouldn't want another.'

Poirot nodded. 'That is how we must do this. Suspect everyone in turn and then cross him or her off the list.'

'How many have you crossed off so far?'

'Not many, Mademoiselle,' said Poirot. 'It depends, you see, on the motive.'

'I don't want to interfere with the official investigation,' said Norman, 'but is there no record of this woman's business affairs?'

Poirot shook his head. 'All the records are burnt.'

'That's unfortunate.'

'*Indeed!* But it seems that Madame Giselle combined a little blackmailing with her moneylending, and that offers other possibilities. Let us say, for instance, that Madame Giselle knew that someone had tried to commit a murder.'

'Is there any reason to suspect that?'

'Why, yes, there is. It is one of the few pieces of clear evidence that we have in this case.' He sighed. 'Ah, well, let us talk of other things. For instance, of how this tragedy has affected the lives of you young people.'

'It sounds horrible, but it has actually done me some good.' Jane told Poirot about her pay rise.

'As you say, but remember, Mademoiselle, your story will only be of interest to people for a very short time.'

'I'm afraid it'll take a bit longer for me,' said Norman, and explained his own position.

'Yes,' agreed Poirot, thoughtfully, 'that is true. Fear may remain for a very long time.'

'Should I keep going?'

'Do you have any other plan?'

'Yes. Close down my practice, go out to Canada and start again.'

'That would be a pity,' said Jane.

Norman looked at her. 'I don't want to go.'

'If I discover who killed Madame Giselle, you will not have to,' said Poirot cheerfully.

'Do you really think you will?' asked Jane.

'If one approaches a problem with order and method, there should be no difficulty in solving it. But I would solve this problem more quickly with help from Mr Gale. And, later on, help from you also.'

'What can I do?' asked Norman.

'I need – a blackmailer.'

'A *blackmailer*?' Norman stared at Poirot. 'What for?'

'To blackmail, of course!'

'Who? Why?'

'*Why* is my business. As for who . . .' Poirot paused for a moment, and then became business-like. 'Here is my plan. You will write a private note to Lady Horbury, asking for a meeting. You will remind her that you both travelled to England on the same aeroplane. You will say that some of Madame Giselle's business documents have passed into your hands. She will agree to the meeting. At the meeting you will say some specific things, which I will tell you to say. And you will ask for ten thousand pounds.'

'You're mad! What if Lady Horbury calls the police? I'll go to prison!'

'The lady will not go to the police, I promise.'

'She may tell her husband.'

'She will not.'

'I don't like it.'

'Do you like losing your patients and ruining your career?'

'No, but . . .'

Poirot smiled at him kindly. 'You do not like to treat a lady badly, is that right? But Lady Horbury is not worthy of such concern. She is, in fact, a very unpleasant woman.'

'I still don't like the idea of blackmailing a woman.'

'Ah, but there will be no blackmail. You will not get the money. You have only to produce a certain effect. And then, I will step in.'

'All right,' sighed Norman. 'I'll do it.'

'Good. This is what you must write. Take a pencil.'

Poirot dictated the letter slowly. '*Voilà*,' he said, when it was done. 'Later I will teach you what you must say. Tell me, Mademoiselle, do you ever go to the theatre?'

'Yes,' said Jane.

'Have you seen an American play called *Down Under*?'

'Yes. About a month ago.'

'Do you remember the part of Harry, played by Mr Raymond Barraclough?'

'Yes. He was very good.'

'You thought him attractive? He was a handsome man*?*'

'Definitely,' laughed Jane. 'But he's a good actor, too.'

'I must go and see him.'

Jane looked puzzled. 'You do jump about between subjects, Monsieur Poirot.'

'No, no, I work with order and method. I assume nothing. I test each suspect in turn, to decide if I shall keep them on my list or remove them.'

'Is that what you're doing?' Jane thought for a moment. 'I see. You've tested Mr Clancy, and you've tested us, and you've taken us all off your list?' She suddenly saw it 'Oh! When you mentioned an attempted murder, was that a test?'

'Yes, Mademoiselle. I mentioned attempted murder and I watched Mr Clancy, I watched you, and I watched Mr Gale. Not one of you reacted to my suggestion in any way – not even by the blink of an eye. I could not be deceived on that point. A murderer can prepare himself to deny any <u>accusation</u> that he already knows about. But that entry in a notebook could not have been known to any of you. So, I am satisfied.'

'What a clever man you are, Monsieur Poirot,' said Jane. 'I shall never know why you are saying things.'

'That is simple. I want to find out things.'

'I suppose you've got very clever ways of finding out things?'

'There is only one really simple way.'

'What is that?'

'To let people tell you.'

Chapter 17 In Wandsworth

Henry Mitchell, who had been the senior steward on the flight from Le Bourget, was just sitting down to supper with his wife when Monsieur Poirot came to see him. Poirot insisted that the Mitchells should continue with their supper. He sat down in a chair, discussed the weather, and then came to the reason for his visit. 'Scotland Yard, I fear, is not making much progress with the murder case,' he said.

Mitchell shook his head. 'How can they, Sir, if none of the people on the plane saw anything?'

'Henry's been so worried about it,' added his wife. 'He can't sleep at night.'

'I feel so guilty, Sir. I should have noticed that the lady was dead when I first took round the bills.'

'It would have made no difference,' Poirot assured him.

'Inspector Japp has asked me, again and again, if anything unusual happened on the way over. I'm worried that I have forgotten something – but I know I haven't.'

'There's one thing I would like to ask you, Monsieur Mitchell,' said Poirot. 'Was everything on Madame Giselle's table in the correct place?'

'When I found her?'

'Yes. The spoons, the forks, the salt pot, and so on?'

'Yes. Everything had been cleared away, except for the coffee cups. I didn't notice anything unusual.'

'It is of no importance. I must also speak with Mr Davis.'

'He's working on the 8.45 a.m. service now, Sir.'

'Has this business upset him much?'

'He's young, Sir. I think he's enjoyed the excitement. People have been buying him drinks and asking to hear about it.'

'Does he have a young lady? No doubt his connection with the crime would be exciting to her.'

'He's seeing the landlord's daughter at the *Crown and Feathers* pub. But she's a sensible girl – she doesn't approve of being mixed up with a murder.'

'She is very wise,' said Poirot, rising to his feet.

★ ★ ★

Poirot found Davis at the *Crown and Feathers* and asked him the same question.

'In the correct place, Sir?' said Davis. 'You mean tidy?'

'I mean, was there something missing from the table – or something present that would not usually be there?'

Davis said slowly, 'There was something. I noticed it when I was clearing up, after the police had gone, but I don't suppose that's what you mean. The dead lady had two coffee spoons in her saucer. It happens sometimes, when we're serving in a hurry. I noticed it because there's a saying that two spoons in a saucer means a wedding.'

'Was there a spoon missing from anyone else's saucer?'

'Not that I noticed, Sir.'

Chapter 18 In Queen Victoria Street

Poirot's next enquiry was at the *Ellis Vale Cement Company*, where James Ryder asked his assistant to show the visitor in.

'Forgive me for disturbing you,' said Hercule Poirot. 'It is about the death of Madame Giselle.'

'Well, what about it? Sit down, won't you? The inspector was round here a few days ago, <u>sticking his nose into my business</u>,' Ryder said, bitterly. 'I have my reputation to think of. I'm in a difficult situation because I was sitting just in front of that woman. If I'd known she was going to be murdered, I wouldn't have taken that flight at all! I don't know, though, perhaps I would.' He looked thoughtful.

'Has good come out of evil?' smiled Poirot.

'Well, I made a nice sum of money from talking to the newspaper reporters.'

'The money was perhaps particularly welcome, since you failed to get a loan in Paris?'

'How did you know that?' demanded Ryder. 'It's true, but I don't want people to hear about it.'

'I can keep a secret, I promise you.'

'So, what did you want to see me about?'

'It is – delicate. I have learned that, although you denied it, you did do some business with this woman Giselle.'

'That's a lie! I never saw the woman. I'd never get mixed up with those high-class moneylenders. They prefer to lend to rich women with gambling debts.'

Poirot rose. 'I apologize. There must be some mistake.'

Ryder had passed his test. As he left, Poirot crossed another suspect off his list.

Chapter 19 Enter and Exit Mr Robinson

Lady Horbury sat in her bedroom in Grosvenor Square, and read the letter for the fourth time.

Dear Madam,

I have inherited some documents which used to belong to Madame Giselle. If you or Mr Raymond Barraclough are interested, I would be happy to visit you to discuss them. Or perhaps you would prefer me to talk to your husband?

Yours truly,
John Robinson.

Damn that lying Frenchwoman, thought Lady Horbury. She had sworn that she would protect her clients if she died suddenly. She would have to see the man, of course. Find out what he knew. Though she had no money to offer him . . .

Quickly, she wrote a reply: *Lady Horbury will see Mr Robinson at 11 o'clock tomorrow morning . . .*

★ ★ ★

Norman Gale was shown into a small room on the first floor of the house in Grosvenor Square. Poirot had helped him create a simple but successful disguise – a red face, a small moustache, and a different parting in his hair – and had taught him exactly what he wished him to say. Now, it was up to him.

'Mr Robinson?' asked Lady Horbury.

'At your service.' He bowed.

'I got your letter.'

'Well, what about it, Lady Horbury?'

'I don't know what you mean.'

'Come, come. Everyone knows how pleasant a weekend at the seaside can be; but husbands rarely agree. I think you know exactly what evidence Giselle had. It's really interesting stuff. Now the question is, who wants it most – you or Lord Horbury?'

'How did you get hold of this – evidence?'

'That's not important. I've got it, that's the main thing.'

'I don't believe you. Show me.'

'Oh, I didn't bring anything with me. I'm not that stupid. If we agree to do business, I'll show you the stuff before you hand over the money. That's fair.'

'How much?'

'Ten thousand pounds.'

'Impossible!'

'Oh, it's wonderful what you can do if you try. I'll give you two days to think about it.'

'I can't get the money, I'm telling you.'

Norman sighed. 'Well, perhaps it's only right Lord Horbury should know what's been going on. But remember that a woman who divorces her husband does not get any of his money, and although Mr Barraclough is a talented young actor, he's not earning very much. So, think about what I said.'

Before the unhappy woman could say a word, he turned and left the room.

★ ★ ★

An hour later, the butler announced the arrival of another visitor. 'A Monsieur Hercule Poirot is here, my lady.'

'Who is he? I can't see anyone!'

'He says that Mr Raymond Barraclough asked him to come.'

'Oh. Very well, show him in.'

The butler went to fetch the visitor, and returned to announce him. 'Monsieur Hercule Poirot.'

Poirot entered and bowed as the butler closed the door. Cicely stepped forward. 'Mr Barraclough sent you?'

'Sit down, Madame.'

She sat and he took a chair near her. 'Madame, I am a friend. I have come to help. You are in much trouble. I am a good detective and I know.'

'A detective?' Her eyes widened. 'I remember – you were on the plane!'

'Precisely. Now, an hour ago, a man came here to blackmail you. He says he has evidence of your affair with Mr Barraclough – evidence which was once owned by Madame Giselle. Now this man offers them to you for, perhaps, seven thousand pounds?'

'Ten.'

'Ah. And you will not find it easy to get that sum very quickly?'

'I can't! I'm in debt already. I don't know what to do . . .'

'Calm yourself, Madame. I, Hercule Poirot, will deal with it.'

'And how much will you want?'

Poirot bowed. 'I shall ask only for a photograph of a very beautiful lady. But you must tell me the truth, Madame – the whole truth – or I cannot help you.'

'And you'll get me out of this mess?'

'You will never hear of Mr Robinson again.'

'All right. I'll tell you everything.'

'Good. So, you borrowed money from Giselle?'

Lady Horbury nodded.

'When did this begin?'

'Eighteen months ago. I had lost a lot of money, gambling.'

'Who sent you to her?'

'Raymond Barraclough. He told me that she lent money to society women. And she did – she lent me as much as I wanted.'

'You and Mr Barraclough had become friends?'

'Yes.'

'But you did not want your husband to know about it?'

'Stephen is tired of me,' Cicely cried, angrily. 'He would like to divorce me.'

'And you did not want divorce?'

'No!'

'You liked your position, and the money. I understand. Let us continue. Madame Giselle wished for repayment?'

'Yes, and when I couldn't pay her back, she became awful. She knew about me and Raymond – places, dates, everything.'

'And she threatened to send this evidence to Lord Horbury?'

'Yes, unless I paid her back.'

'And you couldn't?'

'No.'

'So her death was quite fortunate?'

'It was wonderful!'

'But it made you nervous, perhaps? After all, you were the only person on the plane with a motive for her death.'

She gasped. 'I know. I was in an absolute panic about it.'

'Especially since you had visited her in Paris the night before, and argued with her?'

'The old <u>bitch</u> wouldn't give in. I think she actually enjoyed it.'

'And yet you said at the inquest that you had never seen the woman before?'

'Well, what else could I say? It's been awful. Nothing but lies. That inspector has been here again and again, asking questions.

But he didn't know anything, so I felt quite safe. Until that awful letter yesterday.'

'You have not been afraid that someone would find out? Or that you might be arrested for murder?'

Her face went white. '*Murder?* I didn't *kill* her! Oh, you must believe me. I never moved from my seat.' Her beautiful blue eyes were desperate.

Hercule Poirot nodded. 'I believe you, Madame. Because of the wasp.'

She stared at him. 'A *wasp?*'

'Exactly. Now, then, I will deal with this Mr Robinson, but in return for my help, I will ask you two questions. Was Mr Barraclough in Paris the day before the murder?'

'Yes, we had dinner together. But he thought that I should go and see the woman alone.'

'Ah, did he? One more question: when you were a dancer, your professional name, before you were married, was Cicely Bland. What was your real name?'

'Martha Jebb.'

'And you were born, where?'

'Doncaster. Why?'

'Just curiosity. Forgive me. And now, Lady Horbury, may I give you some advice? Why don't you arrange a divorce with your husband? Once you are free, you can marry a millionaire.'

Cicely laughed. 'Perhaps you are right, Monsieur Poirot.'

Chapter 20 The Three Clues

Hercule Poirot went to Scotland Yard, to see Inspector Japp.

'I have come to ask you for news, my friend,' he said.

'Well, there isn't much. The antique dealer in Paris has identified the blowpipe all right. But the stewards still insist that nothing unusual happened on the flight. And so do the passengers. Not everyone can be lying!'

'Who do you think did it?'

'Well, there are rumours about Dr Bryant and one of his patients. A pretty woman, with a nasty husband. Ryder tried to get a loan in Paris and failed. His company was in real trouble a week or two ago, but seems to be recovering now. Clancy's got something on his mind, but I can't find a motive. And I can't get a word out of Lady Horbury. The whole thing is a mess. I suppose *you've* got it all solved?'

'No, no, there is still far to go. But I have made a little chart.' Poirot took a paper from his pocket. 'My idea is this: a person commits a murder for a particular reason. Suppose you want money. You will get it when an aunt dies. So, you kill the aunt and inherit the money. *Eh*, *bien*, that is that! But in this case, a single murder affects eleven people, with different results.'

He laid out the page. Japp read it over his shoulder:

Miss Grey	Result: improvement. Has gained a pay rise.
Mr Gale	Result: bad. Loss of dental practice.
Lady Horbury	Result: good, if she is CL 52.
Miss Kerr	Result: bad. She is interested in Lord Horbury. If he divorces his wife, he'll be free to marry her. Giselle's death prevents him from receiving the evidence which would allow him to do this.

'Hmm.' Japp looked up from the list. 'You think Miss Kerr is attracted to Lord Horbury? You are very good at discovering secret love affairs.'

Poirot smiled. Japp returned to the paper again.

Mr Clancy	Result: good. Expects to make money by writing a book dealing with the murder.
Dr Bryant	Result: good, if he is RT 362.
Mr Ryder	Result: good, because of cash obtained through newspaper interviews on murder which helped company through delicate time. Also good if Ryder is XVB 724.
Monsieur Dupont, Jean Dupont, Mitchell, Davis	Result: unaffected.

'Mr Clancy, Miss Grey, Mr Ryder, and Lady Horbury all benefit from the death of Madame Giselle,' said Poirot. 'Mr Gale and Miss Kerr lose because of it. Four people are unaffected. And Dr Bryant is either unaffected, or gains something – if he is RT 362. And so, we must continue the hunt. The most interesting thing about this case is the personality of the dead woman. A woman without any personal life. A woman who once loved and suffered, and then walked away to begin her life again.'

'Is there a clue in her past?'

'Perhaps.'

'Well, we certainly need it! There aren't any clues in this case.'

'Oh, yes, there are, my friend. We have the Clue of the Wasp. The Clue in the Passenger's Baggage. The Clue of the Extra Coffee Spoon.'

'A *coffee spoon*?'

'Madame Giselle had two spoons in her saucer.'

'That's supposed to mean a wedding.'

'In this case, it meant a <u>funeral</u> . . .'

Chapter 21 Jane Takes a New Job

Norman, Jane and Poirot met for dinner on the night after the 'blackmailing incident'. Norman was pleased to learn that Poirot no longer needed 'Mr Robinson'.

'He is dead, the good Mr Robinson.' Poirot raised his glass. 'Let us drink to his memory.'

'What happened?' asked Jane.

'I found out what I wanted to know.'

'Was she mixed up with Giselle?'

'Yes. But I wanted the full story.'

'And you got it?'

'Yes, I got it.' Poirot changed the subject and began to discuss the relationship between a career and life. 'It is interesting to note,' he observed, 'that most people will find a job to do that truly makes them happy. You might hear a man who works in an office say that he dreams of travelling the world and exploring other countries. But you will usually find that he is perfectly happy to read books about such adventures, while preferring to work in the safety and comfort of an office.'

'I disagree,' said Gale. 'I'm a dentist by chance, not choice. My uncle was a dentist, and wanted me to work for him. But I wanted to see the world. I gave up dentistry and went to work on a farm in South Africa. But it didn't work out – so, I had to accept the old man's offer and come back to set up business with him.'

'And now you are thinking of giving up dentistry again and going off to Canada.'

'This time I shall be forced to do it.'

'Nothing's forcing *me* to travel,' said Jane sadly. 'I wish it would.'

'*Eh bien*, said Poirot. 'I go to Paris next week. And you can take the job of my secretary. I will give you a good salary.'

Jane shook her head. '*Antoine's* is a good job.'

'So is mine.'

'Yes, but it's only temporary.'

'I will get you another job of the same kind.'

'No, thanks.'

Poirot smiled.

★ ★ ★

Three days later Poirot's telephone rang.

'Monsieur Poirot,' said Jane, 'is that job still available?'

'But yes, Mademoiselle. I go to Paris on Monday.'

'Can I really come?'

'Yes, but what has happened to make you change your mind?'

'I lost my temper with a customer. She was an – an absolute – well, I can't say what she was, but I told her exactly what I thought of her. So, I lost my job. And I'd like to come to Paris with you.'

'Good.'

★ ★ ★

Poirot and Jane travelled to Paris by boat and train. On the way he told her about his plans.

'There are several people in Paris that I have to see. Maître Thibault, Monsieur Fournier, and the two Duponts. Now, Mademoiselle, whilst I am talking to the father, I shall leave the son to you. You are very charming, and I expect that Monsieur Jean will remember you from the inquest.'

'I've seen him since then,' said Jane, and she told Poirot about the meeting in the *Corner House*.

Poirot smiled. 'He attracts you, this young man? He is good-looking, eh?'

Jane laughed. 'That's not how I would describe him. He's very sweet.'

★ ★ ★

Two days later, Poirot and his secretary had dinner with the two Duponts. Jane found Jean just as friendly and easy to talk to as he had been in London, while Poirot and Monsieur Dupont discussed Persian archaeology. Poirot's interest seemed to be real and Monsieur Dupont enjoyed himself enormously. He did not often find such an intelligent and sympathetic listener.

It was suggested that the two young people should go to the cinema. Once they had gone, Poirot's interest suddenly became more practical. 'I imagine it is hard in these difficult financial days to raise enough money to pay for your trips,' he said. 'Do you accept private <u>donations</u>?'

'My friend, we pray for them! But, unfortunately, most people do not care about pottery. They are only interested in paying for archaeological digs that are looking for gold! And yet, the whole of human history can be read through pieces of pottery!'

'Would five hundred pounds be of use?'

Monsieur Dupont nearly fell over. 'You've offering that to me? To help with our research? It is the biggest private donation we have ever had.'

Poirot coughed. 'I would ask one favour. My charming young secretary – could she come with you on your next trip?'

Monsieur Dupont was surprised. 'Well, it might be possible. I will have to ask Jean.'

'Mademoiselle Grey is passionately interested in pottery. It is the dream of her life to go on an archaeological dig. Also, she is very clever with a needle and thread, and can sew on loose buttons.'

'Very useful.'

'Yes, is it not?'

★ ★ ★

At the hotel, Poirot found Jane saying good night to Jean Dupont in the hall. As they went up in the lift he said, 'I have found you a job of great interest. You are to travel with the Duponts to Persia in the spring.'

Jane stared at him. 'Are you mad? I'm not going to Persia. I shall be in Muswell Hill, or Canada, with Norman.'

Poirot smiled gently. 'My dear child, just a possibility. Who knows what may happen between now and then? For me, it is the same – I have offered a donation, but I have not yet signed a cheque! I must buy you a book on Prehistoric Pottery of the Near East in the morning. I have said that you are passionately interested in the subject. I have also said that you sew on buttons perfectly.'

Jane sighed. 'It's not easy being your secretary, is it?'

Chapter 22 Anne Morisot

At half past ten the next morning, Monsieur Fournier walked into Poirot's sitting-room and shook the little Belgian's hand.

'Monsieur, I have, at last seen the point of what you said in London about finding the blowpipe.'

'Ah?' Poirot's face lit up.

'Yes.' Fournier sat down. 'Why was the blowpipe found, when it might easily have been passed out through the ventilator? I think now that the blowpipe was found because the murderer *wanted* it to be found.'

'Bravo!' said Poirot

'That was your meaning, then? Good. So, *why* did the murderer want the blowpipe to be found? The answer: because the blowpipe was not used.'

'Exactly!'

'The poisoned dart was used, but something else was used to send it through the air. Something that a person normally put to their lips, and which would cause no comment. I remembered your list of everything that was found in the passengers' luggage, and two things attracted my attention. Lady Horbury had two cigarette holders, and the Duponts had a number of pottery pipes. Both those things could have been put to the lips naturally without anyone noticing. Am I right?'

Poirot hesitated, 'You are almost there, but you have forgotten the wasp.'

Fournier stared at him. 'The wasp?'

'Yes, I . . .' Poirot stopped speaking as the telephone rang, and picked up the receiver. ''*Allo*? Ah, good morning, Monsieur Thibault. Yes, indeed. Very well. Monsieur Fournier? Yes, he's here.' He turned to Fournier. 'He tried to find you at the Sûreté. They told him that you're here. He sounds excited.'

Fournier took the telephone. '*Allo*, Fournier speaking. What? *Really?* Yes, I am sure he will. We will come at once.'

He put down the receiver and looked at Poirot.

'Madame Giselle's daughter has arrived from America to claim her inheritance.'

'*What?*'

'Thibault has asked her to return at half past eleven. He asks us to go round and see him.'

'Certainly. I will leave a note for Mademoiselle Grey.'

Poirot wrote as follows:

There have been developments. I have gone out. If Monsieur Jean Dupont calls, be pleasant to him. Talk to him of buttons, but not yet of prehistoric pottery.

Hercule Poirot.

★ ★ ★

Maître Thibault welcomed Poirot and Fournier with great pleasure, then turned his attention to the question of Madame Giselle's <u>heiress</u>. 'I received a letter yesterday,' he said, 'and this morning the young lady herself visited me.'

'How old is Mademoiselle Morisot?'

'Mrs Richards – she is married now – is twenty-four years old.'

'Did she bring documents to prove her identity?' asked Fournier.

'Certainly.' Thibault opened a file and took out a copy of a marriage certificate between George Leman and Marie Morisot, both of Quebec, Canada, dated 1910, and the birth certificate of Anne Morisot Leman, as well as other documents and papers.

'It seems that Marie Morisot was a nursery nurse when she met Leman. He left her soon after the wedding, and she went back to using her <u>maiden name</u>. The baby was brought up at the <u>Convent</u> of Saint Marie in Quebec. Marie came to France soon afterwards. She sent money back to Canada for the child, from time to time.'

'How did Anne discover that she was the heiress to a fortune?'

'We advertised in the newspapers. The head of the convent saw one of these advertisements, and sent a telegram to Mrs Richards, who was in Europe, but was about to return to the States.'

'Who is Mr Richards?'

'I understand that he is an American, from Detroit, and makes surgical instruments.'

'He did not come to Europe with his wife?'

'No, he stayed in America.'

'Can Mrs Richards suggest any possible reason for her mother's murder?'

The lawyer shook his head. 'She knows nothing about her. In fact, she did not even remember her mother's maiden name.'

'It looks as though she is not going to be of any help in solving the murder,' sighed Fournier.

The door opened and a secretary announced, 'The lady has returned.'

'Ah,' said Thibault. 'Come in, Madame Richards. May I present Monsieur Fournier of the Sûreté, who is in charge, in this country, of the investigation into your mother's death. And Monsieur Hercule Poirot, who is kindly giving us his help.'

Giselle's daughter was a dark, smartly-dressed young woman. She held out her hand to each of the men in turn. 'I'm afraid, Gentlemen, that I do not feel as a normal daughter would about the matter. I have really been an <u>orphan</u> all my life.' She spoke gratefully of *Mère Angélique*, the head of the Convent of Saint Marie. 'She has always been so kind to me.'

'When did you leave the convent, Madame?' asked Fournier.

'I was eighteen, Monsieur. I went to work for a dressmaker. I met my husband when he was in Nice on business. He came back from the States to Holland and we were married in Rotterdam a month ago. He had to return to the States before me. But I am now about to rejoin him.' Anne Richards' French was fluent and relaxed.

'How did you hear of the tragedy?'

'I read about it in the papers, but I did not know that the victim was my mother. Then I received a telegram from *Mère Angélique*, giving me the address of Maître Thibault and reminding me of my mother's maiden name.'

It was clear that Mrs Richards knew nothing about her mother's life or business affairs. Having written down the address of her hotel, Poirot and Fournier left Maître Thibault's office.

* * *

'You are disappointed, my friend,' said Fournier. 'Did you suspect that the girl might not really be Giselle's daughter?'

Poirot shook his head. 'No. But I have seen her before. I wish I could remember where. Or her face reminds me of someone . . .'

'You have always been interested in the missing daughter.'

'Naturally,' Poirot raised his eyebrows. 'My friend, a very large fortune passes to this girl. From the beginning I thought she might be involved. Miss Venetia Kerr is of a well-known family. But ever since Madame Giselle's maid, Elise, suggested that the father of Madame Giselle's child was an Englishman, I have wondered about the two other women on the plane. I thought one of them might be this daughter. They were both about the right age.'

★ ★ ★

As they entered Poirot's hotel, a man standing at the reception turned towards them and smiled. 'Monsieur Poirot!'

Poirot went forward to shake his hand. 'Dr Bryant! Are your patients managing to do without you for a while?'

The doctor smiled tiredly. 'I have no patients now. I have given up my job, Monsieur Poirot. I love being a doctor, and I am sorry to leave my profession. But, there is a lady – a patient of mine – who I love very much. She is very unhappy in her marriage, but she has no money of her own, so she cannot leave her husband. For some time I didn't know what to do, but now I have made up my mind, and we are on our way to Kenya, to begin a new life. I hope that at last she may know a little happiness. She has suffered so much. I am telling you, Monsieur Poirot, because soon everyone will hear the news, and I wanted you to be the first to know about it.'

'I understand,' said Poirot. 'My best wishes for your future, *Monsieur le docteur,* and for that of Madame.'

Dr Bryant walked off, and Poirot turned to the desk, and asked the receptionist to book a long-distance telephone call to Quebec.

Chapter 23 A Broken Fingernail

'What now?' asked Fournier.

Poirot looked round. 'Ah, here is Mademoiselle Jane. I suggest that you go and begin lunch. I will join you as soon as I can.'

As Fournier and Jane sat down in the dining-room, she asked, 'So, what is Anne Morisot like?'

'Medium height, dark, with a pointed chin. And she is married.'

'Was her husband there, too?'

'No. He is in America.'

Fournier told Jane all about Anne Richards. Poirot joined them as he was finishing the story. 'Well, my friend?' asked Fournier.

'I spoke to *Mère Angélique*. She confirmed that Mrs Richards was brought up at her convent. The mother left Quebec with a French businessman. She sent money for the child regularly, but never suggested a meeting. Anne Morisot left the convent six years ago to become a lady's maid. In that position, she travelled to Europe. She wrote to *Mère Angélique* twice a year. When she saw a report of the inquest in the paper, *Mère Angelique* realized that this Marie Morisot was probably the same Marie Morisot who had lived in Quebec.'

'What happened to Giselle's husband?' asked Fournier.

'His name was George Leman, and he was killed in the early days of the war.' Poirot paused and then said suddenly: 'What did I say? Not in my last comment, but the one before? I believe it was something relevant.' He sighed. 'Ah, well, it is of no importance.'

★ ★ ★

As Jane picked up her bag and gloves at the end of the meal, she gave a little cry of pain.

'What is it, Mademoiselle?' asked Poirot.

'Oh, nothing,' she laughed. 'Just a broken nail. I must file it.'

'Ah, yes! I remember now where I have seen Anne Morisot before . . .' said Poirot quietly. 'In the aeroplane on the day of the murder. Lady Horbury sent her to fetch a nail file. Anne Morisot was Lady Horbury's maid.'

Chapter 24 'I Am Afraid'

Anne Morisot had been at the scene of the crime. Poirot closed his eyes tightly. 'So, I must see how this changes my thoughts on the case.'

'I remember her,' said Jane. 'A tall, dark girl. Lady Horbury called her Madeleine. She sent her to the end of the plane to fetch her a nail file.'

'You mean,' said Fournier, 'this girl went past the seat where her mother was sitting?'

'Yes.'

'Motive and opportunity . . . Yes, it is all there.' Fournier banged the table with his hand. 'But *why* did no one mention this before? Why was she not included with the other suspects?'

'Perhaps because it happened so early? The plane had only just left Le Bourget; and Giselle was alive and well for at least an hour after that.'

Poirot put his head into his hands. 'I must think,' he groaned. 'Can it be possible that my ideas have been completely wrong?'

'My friend,' said Fournier, 'such things happen. Sometimes one must admit one's mistakes and begin again.'

'True,' agreed Poirot. 'Perhaps I thought one particular clue was too important. If I had been wrong – if the item was there just by chance . . . then, yes, I have been completely wrong.'

'For the moment,' said Fournier, 'we must not make Anne Morisot suspicious. She does not know that you have recognized her. We know the hotel at which she is staying and we can keep in touch with her through Thibault. We have identified both opportunity and motive. As for the snake poison – well, the American who bought the blowpipe and <u>bribed</u> Jules Perrot at

United Airlines might be the husband, Richards. We have only her word that he is in the States.'

'Yes, the husband. Ah, wait – wait!' Poirot tightened his hands around his head. Then he let go and sat up very straight. 'If Anne Morisot is innocent, why did she hide the fact that she was Lady Horbury's maid? Anne Morisot has lied. But, if my first theory was correct, would that fit with Anne Morisot's lie? It might, it might . . . But if I am correct, then Anne Morisot should not have been on the plane at all.' Suddenly, he cried. 'Of course! That's it! And it should be simple to find out.' He rose from the table.

'What now, my friend?' asked Fournier.

'I must telephone Lady Horbury in Grosvenor Square. I hope I am lucky enough to find her at home.'

★ ★ ★

Poirot was in luck. Lady Horbury was at home.

'Lady Horbury? It is Hercule Poirot, calling from Paris. No, no, I am not calling about that at all. Can you tell me, please, when you go from Paris to England by air, does your maid usually go with you, or does she go by train? By train . . . And on that particular day? I see. Yes, I see. *Au revoir*, goodbye. Thank you.'

He replaced the receiver and turned to Fournier. 'Lady Horbury's maid usually travelled by train and boat. On the day of Giselle's murder Lady Horbury decided at the last moment that it would be better if Madeleine went by air, too.' He took the Frenchman by the arm. 'We must go to her hotel. If I am correct, Anne Morisot is in great danger!'

★ ★ ★

Poirot and Fournier hurried to the hotel where Anne Morisot was staying. Poirot asked at the reception desk for Mrs Richards, but he was told that she had left half an hour before. Apparently, an American gentleman had called to see the lady. She had seemed surprised to see him. They had eaten lunch together, and then the lady had her luggage brought down, and ordered a taxi to the *Gare du Nord* railway station.

'The *Gare du Nord*,' said Fournier, 'is the station from which you can catch a train to the port of Boulogne. From there, I think she will probably board a boat and sail to England. We must telephone Boulogne and warn them to look for her – and we must also try and find that taxi!'

★ ★ ★

At five o'clock, Jane saw Poirot coming towards her across the hotel lounge. She was going to complain about being left alone at the lunch table, but she stopped when she saw the expression on his face. 'What is it?' she asked, with concern.

'Life is terrible, Mademoiselle,' he sighed. 'When the train arrived in Boulogne they found Anne Morisot dead in a first-class carriage. In her hand was a bottle which had contained hydrocyanic acid.'

'Oh! Was it suicide?'

'The police think so.'

'And you?'

Poirot shrugged his shoulders. 'What else could it be?'

Chapter 25 After Dinner Speech

Jane and Poirot returned to England. When Norman met Jane at Victoria station, he told her that the newspapers had reported that a Canadian lady had committed suicide in the Paris-Boulogne express, but nothing more. There was no mention of any connection with the aeroplane murder. 'The police may suspect her of killing her mother, but they probably won't continue with the case now,' he said. 'And until the general public believes that she is guilty, we must remain suspects ourselves!'

Norman repeated his concern to Poirot when he met him in a London street, a few days later.

Poirot smiled. 'You think I am an old man who achieves nothing! Come and have dinner with me tonight. Inspector Japp and Mr Clancy are also coming. I have some things to say that may be interesting.'

★ ★ ★

At the end of a pleasant meal, Poirot sat back and prepared to speak. 'My friends, Mr Clancy here is interested in the way I work, so I am going to explain to you all my methods in dealing with this particular case.' He paused to look at some notes. 'I will start with the flight of the *Prometheus* from Paris to London. When, just before we reached Croydon airport, Dr Bryant went with the steward to examine the body of the woman, I went with him. Because I, too, have a professional opinion where deaths are concerned. Dr Bryant confirmed that the woman was dead, but he could not confirm the cause of death. Jean Dupont suggested the death was due to allergic shock, following a wasp sting, and showed us a wasp that he himself had killed. This was a believable theory. There was a mark on the woman's neck that looked like a sting. But at that moment I looked down and saw what might have been the body of another wasp. In fact, it was a long thorn, tied with yellow and black thread. Mr Clancy explained that it was a dart shot from a native blowpipe. A blowpipe was later found on the plane.

'By the time we reached Croydon several ideas were working in my mind: the true <u>nerve</u> of one who could commit a crime in such a way; the fact that nobody saw it happen; the wasp; the blowpipe. Why did the murderer not get rid of it through the ventilating hole in the window? The dart might be difficult to identify, but a blowpipe which still had a piece of the price label on it was a very different thing. Obviously, the murderer *wanted* it to be found. If a poisoned dart and a blowpipe were found, everyone would think that the murder had been committed by a dart shot from a blowpipe. But perhaps the murder had *not* been committed that way? The cause of death was certainly the poisoned dart but what is the most successful way to place a poisoned dart in the <u>jugular vein</u>? The answer is, by hand. The blowpipe suggested distance, but if I was right then Madame Giselle's killer had walked up to her table and bent over her. Either of the stewards could have leaned over Madame Giselle, and nobody would notice. Mr Clancy had also passed Madame Giselle's seat – and it was he who first mentioned the blowpipe and dart theory.'

Mr Clancy jumped to his feet. 'I protest!'

'I have not finished, my friend. Neither Mitchell, Davis, nor Mr Clancy seemed likely murderers. So, next, I considered the wasp. It was strange that nobody saw it until coffee was served. I worked out a possible method for the crime. The murderer wanted people to think that Madame Giselle was stung by a wasp and had died of heart failure. The success of that idea depended on whether or not the murderer could get the dart back afterwards. It could be done, as long as the death was not suspicious. This is why he replaced the original red silk with black and yellow thread, in order to make the dart look like a wasp. So, our murderer walks up to the victim, sticks the dart in her neck, and immediately releases the wasp! The powerful poison causes almost instant death, but if anyone noticed a cry, the wasp would explain it. The poor woman had just been stung. But the poisoned dart was discovered before the murderer could collect it. The theory of the natural death is now impossible. So, he hides the blowpipe down the side of a seat, and when the plane is searched it is identified as the murder weapon.

'If the murderer had brought the wasp on to the plane, in order to release it at the right moment to cause a distraction, he must have had something in which to keep it. I examined the contents of the passengers' pockets and hand luggage, and found an empty matchbox in Mr Norman Gale's pocket. *But* Mr Gale had never walked down the aisle. He had only visited the toilet and returned to his seat. It was the right clue on the wrong person. But in fact there *was* a method by which Mr Gale could have committed the crime, as the contents of his briefcase showed.'

'My briefcase?' Norman looked puzzled. 'I don't even remember what was in it.'

Poirot smiled. 'I will come to that. So, I had four people who could possibly have committed the crime: the two stewards,

Clancy and Gale. If I could match a motive to a possibility, I would have my murderer! Who would benefit from Madame Giselle's death? Her daughter, who would inherit a fortune. And certain people who were in Madame Giselle's power. I only knew of one passenger who was definitely mixed up with Giselle. Lady Horbury. She had visited Giselle in Paris the night before, she was desperate, and she knew a young actor who might easily have been the American who bought the blowpipe and bribed the clerk in *Universal Airlines* to ensure that Giselle travelled by the 12 o'clock service. She had the motive, but I did not see how it was *possible* for her to commit the crime; and I could not see a motive for the stewards, Mr Clancy, or Mr Gale.

'Were any of my suspects married – and if so, could one of the wives be Anne Morisot? Mitchell's wife, and the girl that Davis was seeing did not fit the picture. Mr Clancy was not married. And Mr Gale was in love with Miss Jane Grey. I investigated Miss Grey's background, and confirmed that she was not Madame Giselle's daughter.

'The stewards did not benefit by Madame Giselle's death. Mr Clancy was planning to write a book on the subject. Mr Gale was losing patients from his dental business. Apparently he lost, not gained, by the death of Giselle. I decided to get to know him better. I asked him to help me. I involved him in the fake blackmailing of Lady Horbury. He was a good actor and played his part perfectly. Lady Horbury did not recognize him. This convinced me that he could have disguised himself as an American in Paris and also have played the necessary part in the *Prometheus*.

'By now I was very worried about Mademoiselle Jane. Either she was also involved in the crime, or she was completely innocent. And in that case, she might wake up one day to find herself married to a murderer. In order to prevent this, I took her to Paris as my secretary. And while I was there, the missing heiress came to claim her fortune. She reminded me of someone, but I did not realize in time who that person was. The discovery that she had actually been in the plane seemed to destroy my ideas. Here, clearly, was the guilty person. But who was her <u>accomplice</u> – the man who had bought the blowpipe and bribed Jules Perrot? Her husband?

'I saw the answer. But if I was right, Anne Morisot should not have been on the plane. Then Lady Horbury told me that her maid, Madeleine, only travelled in the plane because of a last-minute change of plan.'

'I'm afraid I don't quite understand,' said Mr Clancy

'When did you stop thinking that I was the murderer?' asked Norman.

Poirot turned to him. 'I never stopped. You *are* the murderer. For the last week Japp and I have been busy investigating you. You became a dentist to please your uncle, John Gale, and took his name when you joined his practice – but you were his *sister's* son, and your real name is Richards. It was as Norman Richards that you met Anne Morisot in Nice last winter, when she was there with her employers. She did, in fact, know her mother's maiden name. You identified Giselle in Monte Carlo, and realised that there was a large fortune waiting for Anne if she died. From Anne, you learnt of Lady Horbury's connection with Giselle, and you planned the murder so that suspicion would fall on her. You bribed the clerk in *Universal Airlines* so that Giselle would travel on the same plane as Lady Horbury. You did not expect Anne to be on the plane. It threatened your plans. If anybody found out that Giselle's daughter and heiress had been on the plane, suspicion would naturally fall on her. Your idea was that she should claim her inheritance with a perfect alibi, since she would have been on a train or boat at the time of the crime. Then you would marry her. The girl was in love with you. But you only cared about her money. And at Le Pinet you fell in love with Jane Grey. So, your game became much more dangerous. You wanted to win both the money and the girl you loved. You told Anne Morisot that if she came forward immediately to prove her identity, she would be suspected of the murder. You asked her to take a holiday, and you went together to Rotterdam in Holland, where you married her. Then you told her how to claim the money. She must not mention her job as a lady's maid, and she must make it clear that she and her husband had been abroad at the time of the murder.

'Unfortunately, Anne arrived in Paris to claim her inheritance at the same time as Miss Grey and myself. You were worried that we might recognize Lady Horbury's maid. So you came to Paris yourself, but Anne had already gone to see the lawyer. When she returned, she told you about her meeting with me. Things were becoming dangerous. You had not planned that your new wife would live long after inheriting her wealth. I believe you would have gone to Canada, using the excuse of your failed business, where you would have changed your name back to Richards. Your wife would have joined you there, but it would not have been long before Mrs Richards sadly died, leaving a fortune to her <u>grieving</u> husband. You would then have returned to England as Norman Gale, and said that you had made your fortune by a lucky investment in Canada! But now, this plan was in trouble and there was no time to be lost.'

Norman Gale gave an angry laugh. 'I have never heard such nonsense!'

'Perhaps not. But I have evidence.'

'Evidence as to how I killed Giselle? Everyone knows I never went near her!'

'I will tell you exactly how you committed the crime. You were on holiday. So why did you take a dentist's coat with you? The answer is, because it looked like a steward's coat. When coffee was served and the stewards had left, you went to the toilet, put on your white coat, came out, took a coffee spoon from the <u>pantry</u>, and hurried down the aisle using the spoon as the excuse. You pushed the dart into Giselle's neck, released the wasp from the matchbox, returned to the toilet, changed your coat and walked back to your seat. It only took a couple of minutes. Nobody notices a steward. The only person who might have recognized you was Mademoiselle Jane. But you knew that when a woman is travelling with an attractive man, she will take any chance to look into her hand mirror, and repair her make-up.'

'Anything else?'

'Yes. You once worked on a farm in South Africa. A snake farm.'

Fear showed in Gale's eyes. He tried to speak, but the words would not come.

'They recognized a photograph of you there. The same photograph was identified in Rotterdam as the Richards who married Anne Morisot.'

Norman Gale seemed to change before their eyes. The handsome, confident man had become a rat-like creature, looking round desperately for a way to escape.

'The head of the Convent of Saint Marie made you change your plans when she contacted Anne Morisot. You could not ignore that telegram, but you persuaded your wife that unless she hid certain facts, either she or you might be suspected of murder, because you had both been on the plane when Giselle was killed. As I had been present at Anne's interview in Paris, you were afraid I might discover the truth. Perhaps Anne herself was beginning to suspect you. So you hurried her out of the hotel and onto the train for Boulogne, where you injected her with hydrocyanic acid and left the empty bottle in her hand. You left your fingerprints on the bottle.'

'<u>Damned</u> lies! I wore . . .'

'Gloves, Monsieur? An admission, I think.'

'You damned, interfering little . . . !' Gale ran towards Poirot, his face red with anger. But Japp caught him by the shoulders and held on tightly. 'James Richards, <u>alias</u> Norman Gale,' he said, 'I hold a warrant for your arrest on the charge of murder. I must warn you that anything you say will be taken down and used in evidence.'

* * *

The police took Norman Gale away. Left alone with Poirot, Mr Clancy sighed happily. 'Monsieur Poirot, that was wonderful!'

Poirot smiled. 'Inspector Japp deserves as much credit as I do. He has done great work, identifying Gale as Richards.'

'Poor little Jane Grey.'

'She has courage. She will survive.' Poirot picked up a pile of magazines that Norman Gale had knocked over, and noticed a photograph of Venetia Kerr at a race meeting, "talking to Lord Horbury and a friend". He showed it to Mr Clancy. 'You see that? In a year's time there will be an announcement: "A marriage will shortly take place between Lord Horbury and the Hon. Venetia Kerr." And do you know who will have arranged that marriage? Hercule Poirot! And there is another marriage that I have arranged, too, between Jean Dupont and Miss Jane Grey. You will see.'

★ ★ ★

A month later, Jane came to see Poirot. She looked pale, and tired. 'I should hate you, Monsieur Poirot.'

'If you must. But I think you would rather know the truth than live a lie. And I do not think you would have lived that particular lie for very long. Getting rid of women is a habit that grows.'

'I shall never fall in love again.'

'Naturally.'

Jane nodded. 'But I need to work – I want something interesting to do, to forget about all of this.'

'Then I advise you to go to Persia with the Duponts.'

'But I thought that was only a trick of yours.'

'Not at all. I have become so interested in prehistoric pottery that I sent them the donation I had promised. And they are expecting you to join them on their expedition. Can you draw?'

'Yes. I'm rather good, actually.'

'Excellent. Then you will enjoy yourself.'

'It would be wonderful to get away!' Jane's cheeks grew pink, and she looked at him suspiciously. 'Monsieur Poirot, you're not – being kind?'

'Kind? Mademoiselle, where money is concerned I am strictly a man of business!'

Poirot seemed so offended that Jane apologised for her thought at once. 'Well, then,' she said, 'I'd better visit some museums and look at some prehistoric pottery.'

'*Eh, bien,* that is a very good idea,' smiled Hercule Poirot.

CHARACTER LIST

Jane Grey: a young woman who works in a London hairdressing salon called *Antoine's*, and who recently won some money in a lottery and spent it on a holiday at Le Pinet, on the South Coast of France

Hercule Poirot: a famous Belgian private investigator who is often called in by Scotland Yard to help them to solve difficult murder cases

Lady Cicely Horbury: a beautiful ex-dancer who married Lord Horbury

Lord Stephen Horbury: a wealthy landowner, married to Cicely

The Honorable Venetia Kerr: an aristocratic young lady, well-known in London society

Norman Gale: a handsome young dentist

Madeleine: Lady Horbury's French maid

Dr Roger Bryant: a doctor with many rich high-class patients, and a surgery in Harley Street, in Central London

Armand Dupont: a famous French archaeologist – an expert in ancient pieces of pottery, recently returned from an expedition to Eastern Asia

Jean Dupont: son of Armand Dupont – also a respected archaeologist who always joins his father on his expeditions

Daniel Clancy: a successful writer of sensational detective stories

James Ryder: a businessman – owner of the Ellis Vale Cement Company

Marie Morisot, also known as Giselle: a professional private moneylender who lives in Paris

Henry Mitchell: the senior steward working on board the *Prometheus*

Albert Davis: the junior steward working on board the *Prometheus*

Inspector Japp: head of the English police team at Scotland Yard that is investigating the murder on the *Prometheus* – he has known Hercule Poirot for many years

Constable Rogers: a policeman who works with Inspector Japp

Mâitre Thibault: Marie Morisot's lawyer in Paris

Dr James Whistler: the police surgeon who examined the body of Marie Morisot

Henry Winterspoon: an expert on poisons who works for the government

Detective Sergeant Wilson: part of the team of policeman who searched the *Prometheus*

Monsieur Fournier: a member of the *Sûreté* – the Paris police force – who is leading the team of French policemen investigating the murder on the *Prometheus*

Anne Morisot: Marie Morisot's daughter

Elise Grandier: Marie Morisot's maid

Georges: the doorman at Marie Morisot's home

Monsieur Gilles: the Chief of the *Sûreté*

Monsieur Zeropoulous: a Greek antique dealer with a shop in Paris – Persian antiquities are his speciality

Jules Perrot: an employee at *Universal Airlines* in Paris

Monsieur Antoine: the owner of *Antoine's,* where Jane Grey works

Nurse Ross: Norman Gale's dental assistant

Raymond Barraclough: a handsome young English actor – a close friend of Cicely Horbury

Cultural notes

Air travel in the 1930s

The airport at Croydon to the south of London was the first airport in the world to introduce air traffic control – before London had airports at Heathrow and Gatwick. It opened in 1920.

Le Bourget airport is situated about 11 kilometres to the north east of Paris. It started operation in 1919 and was the only French airport until Orly opened in 1932.

The aeroplanes that flew between Le Bourget (near Paris) and Croydon were small compared to today, and very slow, with propeller engines. Air travel was limited to very few people with the money to travel in this way. It was considered the height of luxury and was a real adventure for people. Air travel was not as safe as it is today, as airplanes had mechanical problems, and could not fly high enough to avoid bad weather. Also radio communications were quite basic then.

Roulette

This is a type of machine used for gambling in casinos. Its name is French for 'little wheel'. It consists of a wheel divided into approximately 37 red or black numbered pockets. The wheel is spun and a ball is thrown in. When the wheel stops spinning, the ball will fall into one of these pockets. Gamblers bet on individual numbers (where they can win the most money), groups of numbers, the colours black or red, or odd or even numbers. In the story, Jane thinks she has bet on number 6 (black) but the winning number is 5 (red).

Blowpipe

This is an ancient weapon used mainly to hunt and kill birds by aboriginal peoples living in jungle areas in South America, Africa and Asia. It looks like a long, narrow tube and is made from the hollow stem of a plant like bamboo. A dart with a sharp point, sometimes dipped in poison to kill larger animals, is blown out of the blowpipe. Because the tube is narrow, the air pressure can make the dart travel up to 30 or 40 metres.

Post mortems and inquests

In the UK, when a person dies the cause of death has to be officially stated in writing by a doctor. If the doctor does not know why the person died – for example, if the death was sudden or suspicious – they ask for a post mortem. This is a medical examination to find out the cause of death, and is usually done by an expert doctor, called a pathologist, who removes the internal organs of the dead person and tests them.

In cases of sudden, violent or suspicious death, it is common to hold a public inquiry called an inquest to find out why the person died. The coroner is the person in charge of the inquest, and the official cause of death is decided by a selected group of twelve ordinary people, called a jury.

At the inquest the coroner and the jury hear medical evidence, as well as evidence from any other people that may be relevant. The family of the person who died and members of the public can also attend the inquest.

Once all the evidence has been heard, the jury gives its verdict – for example, natural death, accidental death, suicide or murder.

The British class system

When this story was written, Britain still had a distinct class system with rules that everybody knew and followed.

It was not generally acceptable for the classes to mix socially and people were expected to have friends and marry someone belonging to the same social class. Lady Horbury had previously been a dancer before she married an aristocrat. She therefore felt socially inferior to Venetia Kerr, who is the daughter of an aristocrat and therefore has the title 'The Honourable'.

This class system lasted until the Second World War (1939–1945) when many social rules changed dramatically, especially in relation to women's role in society, and there began a gradual breaking down of class differences.

Divorce

This is when a married couple legally and permanently separate. In the 1930s, before the law was changed in 1937, a couple who wanted to divorce had to prove that one or the other had been unfaithful. They could not divorce by mutual agreement. One person had to be innocent, and the other guilty of infidelity. This often meant being witnessed in a hotel bedroom with another person, so that evidence could be given in court. This was often deliberately set up, as it was one of the only ways to make sure a divorce was granted. However, it meant telling lies – i.e. committing perjury – in court.

Glossary

Key

n = noun

v = verb

phr v = phrasal verb

adj = adjective

adv = adverb

excl = exclamation

exp = expression

accomplice (n)

a person who helps to commit a crime

accusation (n)

if you make an accusation against someone, you express the belief that they have done something wrong

AD (*Anno Domini*)

used in dates to show a number of years or centuries since the year in which Jesus Christ is believed to have been born

alias (n)

a false name, especially one used by a criminal or actor

alibi (n)

proof that you were somewhere else when a crime was committed

analysis (n)

the process of examining something in order to find out what it consists of

archaeologist (n)

a person who studies ancient societies by looking at what remains of their buildings and belongings

aristocrat (n)
someone whose family has a high social rank, especially someone with a title

arrest (n)
when the police take you to a police station because they believe you may have committed a crime

arrow (n)
a long, thin weapon with a sharp point at one end

baccarat (n)
a card game played in casinos

BC (*Before Christ*)
used in dates to show a number of years or centuries before the year in which Jesus Christ is believed to have been born

big-game (adj)
large wild animals hunted for sport

bitch (n)
a rude name for a woman who behaves in a very unpleasant way

blackmail (n)
threatening to do something unpleasant to someone unless they do what you want them to do

blood is thicker than water (exp)
an expression that means that families are more important than anything else

blowpipe (n)
a tube through which you can blow something – used as a weapon (see Cultural notes)

bribe (v)
to offer an amount of money or something valuable in order to persuade someone to do something

business (n)
used to talk about any activity, situation, or series of events

cigarette-holder (n)
a narrow tube for holding a cigarette

client (n)
someone for whom a professional person or organization provides a service or work

constable (n)
a police officer in Britain of the lowest rank

consultation (n)
a discussion about something

convent (n)
a building in which a community of nuns lives

coroner (n)
the person who is responsible for investigating sudden or unusual deaths

croupier (n)
someone who collects and pays out money in a casino

damn it (excl)
used to express anger or impatience

damned (adj)
a mild swear word which people use to express anger or frustration

dart (n)
a small, narrow object with a sharp point which you can throw or shoot

debt (n)
an amount of money that you owe someone

deceased (n)
a formal word for a person who has recently died

donation (n)
money that you give to help an organization or group

doubtfully (adv)
doing something in an uncertain way

drill (n)
a tool dentists use to make holes in teeth

earl (n)
a man with a high social rank

English Channel (n)
the sea that is between England and northern France

evidence (n)
information from documents, objects, or witnesses, which is used in a court of law to try to **prove** something

fatal (adj)
an accident or illness that causes someone's death

financially (adv)
relating to or involving money

fingerprint (n)
mark made by a person's finger which shows the lines on the skin and can be used to identify criminals

fortune (n)
a very large amount of money

fountain-pen (n)
a pen that is filled with ink

frown (v)
to move your eyebrows together because you are annoyed, worried, or thinking

funeral (n)
a ceremony for the burial or cremation of someone who has died

gambling (n)
betting money on the result of a game, a race, or competition

get rid of (phr v)
to take action so that you no longer have something unpleasant that you do not want

grieve (v)
to feel very sad about someone's death

heiress (n)
a woman who will inherit property, money, or a title

Honourable (adj)
used in Britain in the titles of children whose father is a lord

hunting (n)
chasing and killing animals for food or sport

hydrocyanic acid (n)
a deadly poison

inherit (v)
to receive money or property from someone who has died

inquest (n)
a meeting where evidence is heard about someone's death to find out why they died

inspector (n)
an officer in the British police

involved with (adj)
have a romantic or sexual relationship with

jugular vein (n)
this is in the side of your neck and takes blood from your head back to your heart

jury (n)
the group of ordinary people in a court of law who listen to the facts about a crime and decide if the person accused is guilty or not

justice (n)
the system by which people are judged in courts of law and criminals are punished

laboratory (n)
a building or room where scientific experiments and research are performed

lawyer (n)
a person who is qualified to advise people about the law and represent them in court

legacy (n)
money or property which someone leaves to you when they die

loan (n)
an amount of money that you borrow

lottery (n)
a type of gambling in which people bet on a number or a series of numbers being chosen as the winner

maiden name (n)
a woman's family name before she gets married

mean (adj)
not generous

moneylender (n)
someone whose job is to lend money to people, and usually makes them pay back a lot more money than they borrowed

mortgage (n)
a loan of money from a bank to buy a house

mortuary (n)
a place in a hospital where dead bodies are kept

motive (n)
the reason for doing something

nail file (n)
a thin piece of metal or paper with a rough surface used for making your nails a nice shape

nasal (adj)
sounding as if air is passing through someone's nose as well as their mouth while they are speaking

negotiate (v)
to talk about a problem or a situation in order to solve a problem or complete an arrangement

nerve (n)
the courage you need to do something difficult or dangerous

nonsense (n)
something that you think is untrue or silly

orphan (n)
a child whose parents are dead

pantry (n)
a very small room or a cupboard where food is kept

parachute (n)
a large piece of thin cloth attached to your body by strings which you use to jump from an aircraft and float safely to the ground

Persia (n)
the name used for Iran from ancient times until the early 20th century

place a bet (exp)
money that you risk on the result of a race or game in order to win more money

pottery (n)
objects made from clay

prove (v)
to show that something is definitely true

rear (n)
the back part of something

reputation (n)
the opinion that people have of you

revenge (n)
the act of hurting someone who has hurt you

ridiculous (adj)
very foolish or silly

roulette wheel (n)
a turning wheel used in the gambling game 'roulette,' in which a ball is
dropped onto a wheel with numbered holes in it (see Cultural notes)

safe (n)
a strong metal cupboard with special locks, in which you keep valuable
things

saucer (n)
a small curved plate on which you put a cup

scandal (n)
something that shocks a lot of people because they think it is immoral

Scotland Yard (n)
the London police force that deals with serious crimes

sharply (adv)
doing something in a disapproving or unfriendly way

shiver (v)
to shake slightly because you are cold or frightened

shrug (v)
to raise your shoulders to show that you do not know something

smallpox (n)
a serious disease which leaves marks on your skin

society (n)
used to refer to the rich, fashionable people in a particular place who meet socially

soothingly (adv)
doing something in a gentle way that makes people feel calm

spread out (phr v)
to arrange something over a surface, so that all of it can be seen or used easily

stab (v)
to push a knife or sharp object into something

stained (adj)
becoming coloured or marked by a liquid

stick your nose into somebody's business (exp)
to become interested or involved in something that does not concern you

sting (n)
when an insect pricks your skin, usually with poison, so that you feel a sharp pain

suicide (n)
the act of deliberately killing yourself

sun worshipper (n)
someone who likes to lie in the sun

surgeon (n)
a doctor who does operations

surgery (n)
the room or house where a doctor or dentist works

suspect (v)
to believe that something is true but you want to make it sound less
strong or direct

tart (n)
a very insulting word for a woman who you think is too friendly with men

theory (n)
if you have a theory about something, you have your own opinion about
it which you cannot prove but which you think is true

thorn (n)
a sharp point on a plant

thread (n)
a long, thin piece of cotton, silk, nylon, or wool

tragedy (n)
an extremely sad event or situation

tribe (n)
a group of people of the same race, language, and customs, especially
in a developing country

unconscious (adj)
a state similar to sleep, as a result of a shock, accident, or injury

verdict (n)
the decision that is given by the jury or judge at the end of a trial

victim (n)
someone who has been hurt or killed

wasp (n)
a small insect with a painful **sting** which has yellow and black stripes
across its body

will (n)
a document where you say what you want to happen to your money and
property when you die

witness (n)
a person who saw an accident or crime

yard (n)
a length of 36 inches or approximately 91.4 centimetres

THE AGATHA CHRISTIE SERIES

Visit **www.collinselt.com/agathachristie** for language
activities and teacher's notes based on this story.